BOOKS BY BARBARA CORCORAN

# FACE THE MUSIC

# FACE THE MUSIC

## BARBARA CORCORAN

Atheneum    1985    New York

*Library of Congress Cataloging in Publication Data*

*Corcoran, Barbara.*
*Face the music.*

*SUMMARY: Marcie finds help in her guitar and*
*bluegrass music when she needs to break away from*
*her overprotective divorced mother.*
*[1. Mothers and daughters—Fiction] I. Title.*
*PZ7.C814Fac 1985 [Fic] 85-7453*
*ISBN 0-689-31139-7*

*Published simultaneously in Canada by*
*Collier Macmillan Canada, Inc.*
*Composition by Maryland Linotype, Baltimore, Maryland*
*Printed and bound by Fairfield Graphics,*
*Fairfield, Pennsylvania*
*Designed by Scott Chelius*
*First Edition*

To Lisa Rogers, without whom, as they say, there would have been no book. That beautiful guitar you hear in the background is hers.

# FACE THE MUSIC

Marcie noticed the little wriggle her grandmother gave and smiled. When Nana squirmed like that, it meant she was especially interested, and now she was leaning forward a little, listening intently to Father Goodhue's sermon.

Marcie always forgot when she had been away how small her grandmother was. Her feet barely touched the floor, and she seemed to stretch upward as if to hear better.

On Marcie's other side, her mother was gazing around at the congregation with a vague little smile, as if she wanted to be sure of looking pleasant if anyone caught her eye. She was not, as far as Marcie could tell, listening to Father Goodhue.

The tall forty-year-old priest was talking in his quiet voice about anger. He spoke of what Jesus said about it in the Sermon on the Mount, and what psychologists said about the dangers of suppressing it. Marcie had been away at college when Father Goodhue's wife left him, but her mother had written her that he had taken it hard. He was saying now, ". . . and you know I don't often speak of my own feelings, but I would like to tell you something that happened to me. A few weeks ago I stood at the altar ready to begin the service, and I felt as if I would drown in the wave of anger and bitterness that swept over me. I thought, 'God, I cannot deal with this. You will have to help.' " He paused and looked down at the lectern. The church was very still. "You know I am not by nature a mystic. But by the end of that service I was at peace." He turned away, making the sign of the cross and murmuring the familiar words.

Marcie was touched. She did not know him well. He had come here during her last year of high school, and he was a reserved man, not easy to know. But she liked him and respected him. Now suddenly she saw him differently, as a man who suffered. She was eighteen and only lately had she begun to see adults as people in their own right. She glanced sideways at her mother, trying to see her as someone quite separate from herself. But that was harder. Her mother made it harder, by attaching herself so tenaciously to Marcie. She thought of the day, during her first month in the dorm, when her mother had come into Boston on the train and had come to see her unannounced. Marcie had stood at the top of the stairs looking down at her mother in the dorm hall and had had the weirdest sense of looking at another aspect of herself. The impression had stayed with her all day and made her nervous.

4

After the communion service and the choir's recessional hymn, she knelt a moment and then stood up, smiling at her grandmother. Her mother was already in the aisle talking to friends.

Outside the small fieldstone church, Marcie and her grandmother waited.

"Nana," Marcie said, "you're looking great."

"For my age, you mean." Her grandmother gave her a mischievous grin. "You mean I'm well preserved."

Marcie laughed. "I don't mean that, and you know it."

"Well, I'm getting old, and frankly, it bugs me." Nana glanced at her watch. "Have you ever estimated how many minutes, hours, even days we have spent in our lifetime waiting for your mother? Let's go get a booth at Woodbury's. She'll find us."

When they were settled in the booth, she said, "You've got something on your mind."

"How do you always know?"

"I'd love to say because I'm psychic, but in fact it's always written all over your face. You will never succeed in any career that requires deception."

Marcie took a deep breath. "I've made a big decision. I'll wait till Mom gets here so I only have to say it once. It's kind of scary."

"All right. Let's have the complete brunch, shall we? I'm starved. I love to prowl around that buffet table, piling up my plate with fattening food. Be sure to try the creamed chipped beef. They put sherry in it." She nodded and smiled at the waitress who was filling the coffee cups. "We're going the pig-out route."

The waitress laughed. "Good for you, Mrs. Evans."

Marcie kept glancing at the door, nervous about telling her mother what she had decided. It might be easier to tell her with Nana here. Nana always supported her. "Nana, you look awfully cute in that blue pant suit. It matches your eyes."

"It's indecent to call a seventy-year-old woman cute, but thank you, darling."

"You look more like fifty."

"That makes me feel as if I've done something remarkable that I have to sustain. I want to be able to look seventy when I feel seventy. Here comes your mother."

Marcie watched her mother's smiling progress between the tables. She stopped several times to chat with people she knew. She belonged to three bridge clubs and the church Women's Guild and several other groups that Marcie kept losing track of.

"I couldn't find you." She slid into the seat next to Marcie.

"We aren't good waiters," Nana said.

"I know that all right." She gave Nana a mildly reproachful glance. "But so many people wanted to say hello to you, Marcie. Your first Sunday back."

"I said hello to about a hundred people, Mom," Marcie said.

"Well, let's eat," Nana said. She got up and headed for the long table.

"Mother is so abrupt," Marcie's mother said. She took a sip of her coffee.

"She's hungry. Me too. Want me to get you yours?"

"No, I'll get it." She took out a small mirror and gave her face and hair a quick scrutiny. "I look a fright." She always said that.

"You look fine, Mom." Marcie got up and went to the table to get her plate.

When they were settled with their food in front of them, Nana said, "How did you like the sermon?"

"Poor man," Marcie's mother said, "I feel so sorry for him."

Nana frowned. "Don't, Marian."

"But the poor man is so devastated by his divorce, it's pathetic."

"My father used to say," Nana said, "sympathy is in the dictionary between shit and syphilis."

Marcie laughed and choked on a piece of croissant. Her mother glanced quickly around to see if anyone had overheard. Her mouth tightened into a thin line, and the lines that ran from her nose to the corners of her mouth deepened.

"Mother, you're being revolting," she said in a low voice.

"I often am," her mother said. Then in a softer tone she said, "Marian, don't patronize Norman Goodhue. You know yourself how odious that can be."

Marian's face tightened still more. "I am not enjoying this conversation, and if we can't sit here and—" She broke off, quick tears springing to her eyes. "Perhaps I should go."

Marcie put her hand on her mother's arm. "Relax, Mom. It's okay."

Nana said, "I'm sorry if I upset you. Marcie has something to tell us. Let's hear what it is, Marcie."

It was not the way Marcie had planned to break the news. She should have known, though. Nana and her mother never got along, although both of them tried. And Nana was not one for subtle diplomacy. Well, there was nothing for it now but to get it over with. She took a swallow of coffee. "I'm not going back to college in the fall."

"Oh, my God!" her mother said. "You've flunked out."

"No, no, no. I've got a four-point average. You know that.

7

And I'm not dropping out for good. I just want a year off, to kind of get my head together."

Her mother's expression changed. "You'll be at home. Oh, Marcie, I do think it's a good idea. Listen, why don't we plan Christmas in London? I've been wanting for years—"

"Mom, hold it. I can't live at home."

"But why not? It wouldn't cost you a cent, and we could have such good times, just you and me—"

"Mom. Listen. I want to spend the year doing something with music. You know that group I've been playing with around Cambridge. Well, we might get together and get serious. I don't know yet. It's all tentative. But I want to do something like that."

"Well, I can't say I think much of the music part. I mean, not that kind of music. I suppose your father put you up to it."

Marcie sighed. "Dad doesn't even know about it."

"But he will. He'll have some brilliant idea about you moving in with Ellen and him. He always wanted you to play something, like the way he wasted years trying to play his stupid banjo—" She broke off suddenly, switching to a public smile as a middle-aged couple paused at the table to say hello. As soon as they had gone, she said, "He's still trying to get you away from me."

Marcie was holding onto the edges of her seat trying to hang onto her temper. "Mother, he knows nothing about it. I have no idea of moving in with him. I want to be on my own."

Her mother began to cry, slow, silent tears. Her face squinched up as she fought to control herself. She threw down her napkin, tossed her Visa card on the table, and left.

Marcie pushed back her chair, but Nana held out a restraining hand. "Let her go."

"But I've upset her. I can't just . . ."

"Yes, you can. Sit down, Marcie."

Marcie sat down. She felt like crying herself. "What's so terrible about taking a year off?"

"It isn't that. She's afraid she's going to lose you. That's how she thinks of it—losing you. She's afraid to let you grow up."

"But I've been gone a year."

"Only a forty-minute train ride away. You came home often. She came in town to see you often. Now you might really take off."

"I guess she sees it like Dad leaving her. But Nana, I'm her kid. I mean I'm not married to her."

"Exactly. So go your way. I don't mean to sound hard on your mother, but Marian never grew up."

"I don't know, I don't know. I can't stand it to hurt her any more than she's already been hurt."

"Sweetie, people have to deal with their own hurts. You can't do it for them." She spread marmalade on a piece of toast. "I wish you wouldn't call me Nana."

Marcie looked up in surprise. "I thought you wanted us to."

"It was your mother's idea. It makes me feel like the dog in *Peter Pan*."

"But what should I call you?"

"Why not Jane? It's my name."

Marcie thought about it. "I don't know if I could get used to it."

"Try. And Marcie, remember that an eighteen-year-old girl is not responsible for her mother, beyond the demands of common decency and affection. If necessary, get angry. Now, are you going to Peg's wedding?"

"Of course. I'm a bridesmaid. Peg's friend Kate is maid of honor. You're coming, aren't you?"

9

"Wouldn't miss it. I've never been to Austin."

"Mom's going to fly, but I'm going to drive. I haven't been anywhere except here to Boston since Dad gave me the car. I can't wait. Want to drive with me?"

"Once I'd have jumped at the chance, but I'll fly. I don't do long car trips any more. Not if I can help it."

"At least you've done it. You've been everywhere."

"Not quite." She picked up Marcie's mother's Visa card, gave it to Marcie, and took out money for the bill.

After she had dropped off her grandmother at her apartment house, Marcie drove home the long way, along the Ipswich River, through woods and fields that were lushly green in mid-June. It was good to be home, but she didn't want to stay here. Nana . . . Jane . . . was right in a way, but she couldn't just ditch her mother either. Some kind of compromise would have to be worked out. Mom would get used to the idea if she went at it gradually.

She put a Malvina Reynolds tape in her tape deck and sang along with her. "Don't push me, I'm headed my way, Don't block my highway . . ." She'd like to be able to write her own songs and sing them, the way Malvina had. Maybe someday.

She thought about Ossipee Joe the itinerant banjo player from New Hampshire that her friend Vin had introduced her to. Joe roamed the Appalachian country, picking up with other musicians wherever he found them, playing his bluegrass music. He never stayed put long enough to be part of a permanent group.

He had taught her some bluegrass in the short time he had been in Cambridge. Once he came to the house to give her a special pick he'd bought for her. Her mother had answered the doorbell and had nearly gone into shock when this scruffy-looking bearded man—a hobo, she called him—had asked for her daughter. She had carried on about it for weeks. Maybe Joe did look like a bum, but he made his own way in the world, and he could play the birds off the trees. And he had a heart as big as his Ossipee Mountains.

The boards of the old wooden bridge rumbled as she drove across. She thought of Old Brownie, the horse she had had when she was a kid, who refused to step foot onto that bridge. Caution. Maybe caution was a good thing, but Old Brownie never saw all that was on the other side of the bridge. Hey, she told herself, I'm a philosopher. Okay, Marcie my girl, brace yourself for the other side of the bridge.

# 2

Her mother was sipping a cup of coffee at the kitchen table. There were delicious smells of roasting duck.

"Smells wonderful." Marcie glanced sidelong at her mother to see if she were sulking over the brunch incident. There wasn't any sign that anything had happened. Marcie marveled, as she often had, that her mother could be cooking in a hot kitchen and still look cool and perfectly coiffed. When she herself did anything, her hair always seemed to get totally messed up.

Her mother got up to baste the duck and check on the potatoes.

"What can I do to help?"

"Not a thing. It's all under control." She always said that. She liked to have Marcie clean up afterward, but she would never let her help with the cooking. Cooking was her show, and she was good at it.

She chatted to Marcie about a woman in church who was going to have a mastectomy and about another couple who were thinking of adopting a child. Marcie half-listened. She was thinking about how her mother never went to answer the door without first looking in the hall mirror to check on her appearance. In a way, it was funny, but also it was sad. She thought she was an unattractive woman, but in fact she was rather pretty. When Dad ditched her for Ellen, Marcie thought, that really tore it. Ellen was ten years younger and very attractive. Mom liked to harp on the fact that Ellen tinted her hair and used too much makeup. How sad not to feel good about yourself. Why did a woman feel she had to be beautiful? Her mother had a lot of charm. People liked her. But it was never enough. Maybe because she had once wanted to be an actress, she was always "on."

After her mother went upstairs, Marcie looked at herself in the kitchen mirror. She didn't look at all like her mother or her grandmother. She was tall, with long arms and legs, brown hair, grey eyes like her father's. God knows I'll never win any beauty contests, she told her reflection, but the difference between me and Mom is, I don't give a damn.

The phone rang, and she reached for it. Her mother had answered upstairs, and they said "hello" at the same moment. Marcie started to hang up, but then she heard her sister's voice. "Peg!"

Simultaneously her mother was saying, "Is that you, Margaret? How you startled me."

13

"Sorry, Mom," Peg said, not sounding sorry. "I wanted to check with you both on dates and things. What day are you flying down?"

"The tenth," her mother said promptly. "Will you meet me at the airport? I suppose Austin does have an airport?"

"Mother, you know it does. You've already got your ticket, haven't you? You have to change at Dallas-Fort Worth. What time does your flight get in here?"

Her mother sounded weary. "I don't know, dear. I'll have to check on it and call you back."

"Peg," Marcie said, "I'm going to drive down."

"Good for you. That's great." Peg sounded enthusiastic. "You'll have fun. Doing it by yourself?"

"Yes. Nana's going to fly, and I don't know what Dad's plans are."

"I already talked to him."

"Really," her mother said, distantly. "He's coming alone, I hope?"

"Mom. Of course he is. You didn't think he'd bring Ellen, did you? After all!"

"One never knows."

"Marce?" Peg said.

"Here."

"I just had a brainstorm. Kate will still be in Chapel Hill. Why don't you pick her up and bring her with you?"

There was a click on the phone as their mother hung up.

"Oh-oh," Peg said.

"Never mind," Marcie said. "Listen, I'd love to. I've been wanting to meet Kate for years."

"I'll arrange it and let you know."

"Wonderful. How's my brother-in-law?"

14

Peg giggled. "Perfect. He can't wait to see you."

"Me too. Hug him for me."

"I will. I'll be in touch, babe." Peg rang off.

Marcie put the phone down, smiling. She and Peg had fought and argued and upstaged each other for years before Peg went off to college. Then, somewhere along the way, they had become good friends. Five years older, Peg had gone to the West Coast to college, "as far away as she could get" from the family squabbles. Then she had gone to Austin, Texas, with her roommate, Kate, to UT graduate school and had fallen in love with Kate's cousin.

Kate. Marcie had heard so much about her. She made a face, thinking about the fuss her mother would make if she picked up Kate. Her mother had met Kate only once, but for reasons that Marcie didn't understand, she had taken a violent dislike to her. Oh, well. Mom would just have to accept it. She was Peg's dearest friend, after all, and she was going to be maid of honor at the wedding. And Marcie couldn't wait to meet her.

The phone rang again, and this time her mother didn't answer. It was Vin, just home from college himself, suggesting an afternoon at the beach. He would bring the picnic lunch. She accepted happily, and only after she had hung up did she think of the duck. Her mother would have a fit if she was not home for dinner. She hesitated, her hand on the phone. No, damn it, she was not going to call him back and cancel just for a stupid duck. She would eat cold duck when she got home. Mom would be mad, but she hadn't seen Vin since Easter break. She sighed, wishing she didn't always have to feel guilty about everything.

# 3

"You make super sandwiches," Marcie said. She was sitting with her back against a rock, her legs covered with sand. The hot sun was relaxing. She could still taste salt on her lips from her swim.

Vin popped the last of his chicken salad sandwich into his mouth and took a long drink from his bottle of Anchor Steam beer. "I'll make somebody a wonderful wife."

They had talked nonstop all the way from Marcie's house to the beach, comparing college experiences, swapping impressions. She had known him since kindergarten, and she was very fond of him. People in town said they "went together," but she knew him so well, he was more like a brother than a boyfriend.

She leaned forward and brushed some sand out of his thick curly hair. "Heard anything from Ossipee Joe?"

"Nary a word. Not even the occasional postcard."

"I hope he's okay."

"Me too. But Joe usually lands on his feet. Hey, how about dinner in Rockport tonight? The Blacksmith Shop? And there's a good movie at the Strand."

"I'd love it, but I can't."

"Another date?"

"No, Mom is doing a special homecoming dinner for me. I've already put it off till seven, but if I don't show up at all, she'll have a fit."

"Still on that trip?"

"What trip?" She sounded more defensive than she meant to, because she knew what he meant.

"Feeling guilty because your dad ditched your mom. It wasn't you that did it, Marcie. You're going to screw up your life if you go on feeling responsible for your parents. They aren't your problem."

She didn't want to talk about it. "Ask me to dinner next week, any night at all. I haven't been to the Blacksmith Shop since the last time I went with you. Remember the baked stuffed lobster?"

"You're changing the subject, but all right. Let's make it Wednesday."

She was relieved that he didn't want to go on with a discussion of her family problems, but her feeling of euphoria was gone.

When she told him about Peg's wedding and her plan for driving to Texas, he nodded. "That sounds great. What you ought to do is stay down there."

"Texas?"

"Why not? Austin is a nice city, they say, and there's good music. Not to mention UT if you get a craving for academia. Maybe you could tie up with a couple of other people and play some gigs." Vin himself played drums with a group at college.

"Vin, I can't spend my life playing bluegrass."

"Look, you're eighteen years old. Who's talking about spending your life? Now is the time to do what you really want to do. You can worry later about spending your life."

She was thinking about what he had said when she sat down to dinner with her mother.

"Whew." Her mother pushed the hair back off her forehead and took off her apron. "I hope it's good. It took me all day."

Marcie remembered to say, "It looks marvelous, Mom. Smells heavenly."

"You seem abstracted, dear."

"Not really."

"Did you have a nice time at the beach?" Her mother sat down and began to carve the duck.

"Especially nice. It was good to see Vin."

"Really?" Her mother sounded politely incredulous.

Marcie gave an exasperated little laugh. "Mom, you're so transparent."

"I am?"

"You never have thought much of Vin. You can't believe I had a good time with him."

Her mother gave her attention to the dressing. "This is a special orange dressing. I hope you like it. I'm sure Vin is a perfectly nice boy."

"Damning with faint praise." Marcie felt annoyed, but it was better to turn it into a joke.

"You're making something out of nothing. I didn't say a word about Vincent."

"But you never liked him."

Her mother gave her a winning smile. "Honey, he's so *short*."

"Shit," Marcie said under her breath.

Her mother frowned and put down the serving spoon with a clatter. "If that's the kind of language you learn from your friends, you'd do better to stay at home."

Marcie sucked in her breath. "I didn't learn it from Vin, if that's what you mean. And do we have to have this conversation?"

"Certainly not. You began it, I believe."

They ate in silence for a while. She knew Vin and Nana were right, she really had to get out of here. But what would her mother do all alone in this big house? She counted the days till Marcie came home from college. She planned great meals for her, devoted her time to her, talked to her, listened to Marcie's experiences as if she could hug them tight to herself and make them her own. It was crazy, it was all wrong, but Marcie was all she had. Maybe if she could find a pad in Cambridge and come home weekends this year . . .

She finished her dinner without tasting it.

"You've lost your appetite," her mother said.

She started to say she had eaten at the beach, but she realized that wouldn't help any. "It's the quality, not the quantity," she said, and thought what a stupid remark that was.

"Your grandmother's getting awfully deaf, isn't she," her mother said, finishing her dish of Indian pudding.

"I didn't notice it. At all."

"Well, she is, but she's too proud to have her ears checked. Won't consider a hearing aid."

"Leave her alone, Mom. She's fine."

Her mother gave a small, strained laugh. "There you go, two days home and critical of me already."

"Mom, I'm not—" Marcie made herself stop. From long experience she knew how easily this could turn into one of those arguments she always lost. Her mother would feel persecuted; she would cry and be silent for the rest of the day. Marcie didn't need that. "I'll clean up," she said, getting to her feet.

"I think I'll lie down. I'm starting one of my headaches."

Marcie never knew when and when not to believe in the headaches. Her father always said it was Marian's ultimate weapon, the sure-fire way to triumph in an argument. But sometimes Marcie knew they were real. She could tell from her mother's pale face. Oh, hell, she thought, and slammed the dishes into the dishwasher.

# 4

"Your mother's going to be lonesome," said Mrs. McGraw, who lived next door and somehow managed to be in on everything in the neighborhood.

Marcie was ready to take off. She put some books on the back seat and moved the canvas bag to make room for the guitar.

" 'I dwell but in the suburbs of her pleasure,' " her mother said airily.

Marcie gave her a look half-impatient, half-amused. "It's only for five days, you know, till you come down yourself."

"Five days can be a long time," Mrs. McGraw said dolefully, "when your loved ones are gone."

They were a good pair, Marcie thought, Mrs. McGraw

21

with her never-failing cliché, Mom with her garbled Shakespeare. Her mother had studied acting when she was young, and she always spoke wistfully of the career she gave up, although Nana had told Marcie once that she never did get anything more than a walk-on.

"In her mind," Nana said, "she was Lana Turner, waiting to be discovered in Schwab's drugstore. Only she really wasn't Lana Turner, you see, and the Rexall drugstore where she worked one winter did not attract talent scouts."

Marcie didn't mind if her mother wanted to think of herself as an actress who gave it all up for husband and child. She even looked at the scrapbooks, pictures mostly of school productions and a couple of local shows put on by the Mothers Club. The trouble was, she made too much of her supposed sacrifice.

She kissed her mother, shook hands with Mrs. McGraw, and got into the car.

"Have you filled the tank?" her mother asked. It was a delaying tactic.

"Of course, Mom."

"Do you have your toothbrush?"

"Mother!"

Her mother had the grace to laugh. "Well, I always forget mine. I must have a dozen toothbrushes that I've had to run out and buy when I was away overnight."

Marcie smiled and rolled up the window. "See you." She waved and drove off, careful not to hear whatever her mother's last instructions were. She waved, and then waved again at the corner. Her mother and Mrs. McGraw still stood in the road, waving. When it came to waving, her mother had met her match in Mrs. McGraw, who waved her middle-aged son off to work every morning as if he were setting out for the moon.

She heaved a sigh of relief as the turn in the road left them out of sight. Now she could relax. And Mom and Mrs. McGraw could go in and have another cup of coffee. Mrs. McGraw would sympathize with Mom about having children who were always taking off for somewhere. Marcie had already heard Mrs. McG. on the subject of Peg, first going clear across the country to college, "as if there weren't good schools right here in Massachusetts," and then, horror of horrors, settling and marrying in Texas. "Thank goodness," Mrs. McGraw had said many times, "my Ray loves his home. Nothing could make him leave."

Of course Ray would never leave. He was spoiled rotten at home, everything done for him right down to his mother's devoted ironing of his undershirts.

Forget the McGraws. Forget, for now, Mom and her big brown eyes that filled with tears so quickly and often. Marcie turned on the tape deck and began to smile as a Sarah Vaughan version of Beatles songs filled the car. "The Long and Winding Road" for sure! She sang along with Vaughan as the shiny red Escort rumbled the planks of the old wooden bridge on the shortcut to the Newburyport Turnpike.

# 5

Marcie waited nervously in the lobby of the motel. It was ten minutes past ten. What if Kate had forgotten all about her? What if she had changed her mind and flown back to Texas? But of course she would have left a message. How would they recognize each other? There were a lot of people milling around the lobby, some checking out, some greeting each other, some just standing and waiting. Carefully she examined all the young women who seemed to be alone. There were five of them. She had almost settled on a small, dark-haired woman standing near the door, and she was getting up her nerve to approach her and say, "Are you Kate?" when a man came in from the street, the woman embraced him, and off they went.

I should have stayed in my room, Marcie thought. She may be trying to call me. She ought to check with the operator. She got up and started toward the desk, but at that moment there was a commotion. A little boy coming rather fearfully through the door fell headlong into the lobby. A tall young woman behind him exclaimed and stooped to pick him up. He began to howl, more in fright than in pain. The woman holding him looked distressed. She was striking-looking, with short, curly dark hair and large green eyes. She was saying, "I'm so sorry, darling. Are you all right?"

Another woman came in just behind them, and the woman with the boy turned to her. "I'm terribly sorry. I stepped on his heel. Is he all right, do you think?" She handed the little boy to the other woman.

The second woman hugged the child and said, "Did you get a bump, Tommy?"

He stopped crying and buried his head against her shoulder. The woman smiled at the first young woman. "I'm sure he's all right."

"I'm so sorry."

"He's fine, really. It wasn't your fault. What do you say, Tom—do you think you're ready for pancakes?"

He lifted his head and gave her a tremulous smile. "Yes."

"He's fine." The mother put the child down and took his hand, and they walked toward the restaurant.

The younger woman watched for a moment, then turned in a swift movement toward the desk. She stopped short when she saw Marcie. She looked at her intently for a moment and then said, "You're Marcie."

Marcie had been so absorbed in the little scene with the

child that it had not occurred to her that this might be Kate. "Kate?" she said.

Kate gave her a sudden brilliant smile. "The same. Charging in here late as usual, knocking down little children in my path. It's so good to see you." She held out her hand.

Marcie's nervousness melted. That strong handshake, that smile were reassurance enough. "Me too," she said. "I mean I'm awfully glad to meet you. I didn't know what you looked like. I've seen some snapshots but they weren't very clear . . ."

"I know. Someday Peg should have an exhibition of her photography. Call it 'The World As I See It.' Somehow she manages to make everything look surreal. Have you had breakfast?"

"Yes. Have you?"

"It seems like hours ago. Why don't we have a cup of coffee before we set out?"

"Fine." Marcie followed Kate into the coffee shop, wondering how in the world her mother could have disliked such an attractive person. Nana had said once that Marcie's mother didn't like women who were richer or prettier than she was, but surely Mom wouldn't be so petty . . . She moved forward to hear what Kate was saying.

". . . up half the night packing. I wish I were organized, like Peg. She's ready weeks ahead of time."

"I know."

"I pack on my way out the door, more often than not." She sat down and smiled at Marcie. "It's good to meet you."

"Oh, it's good to meet you, too. I've wanted to for years."

They ordered their coffee.

"I'm going to miss Chapel Hill," Kate said, looking out the window. The motel was on the edge of town, and there was a grove of longleaf pines across the road, the needles rippling in the breeze. "It's a great town."

"What have you been doing here?"

"Some last minute research on my dissertation. My grandmother went to school here in the depression, and I wanted to see if I could get some oral histories. She worked for Roosevelt's relief program, the CWA, the granddaddy of federal relief programs. She used to bounce around the country in her little Model A Ford, giving out sacks of flour and sugar to people who had literally nothing." She shook her head. "Flour and sugar. Can you believe it? I found one very old blind black man still living in a tiny shack that used to be a schoolhouse. It was already abandoned when he was a boy, and his whole family grew up there. He was wonderful, talked to me for hours and played his fiddle for me. Been blind all his life and has lived alone for years." Her eyes had a far-off look, as if she still saw him.

I don't know anything, Marcie thought. "I've lived such a narrow life," she said.

Kate brought her gaze back to Marcie's face. "Honey, you're only . . . what? . . . eighteen?"

"A third of my life is over."

"Make it a fourth." Kate raised her coffee cup. "To the other three-fourths."

Marcie felt better. "Peg was right about you."

"She's right about John, I'll say that for her. He's my favorite relative, next to my mother."

"I'm so glad they're getting married." But what she was really thinking about was Kate's saying that her mother was her favorite relative. So it was okay to be close to your mother. She wondered what Kate's was like.

27

"Before I forget . . . I've got some friends who live in Metaire . . . that's in New Orleans. They want us to spend the night with them. Is that okay with you?"

"Sure, of course."

"There's a bluegrass and country music festival going on. I thought you might like that."

Marcie gasped. "Wow! I'd love it! I've never been to a real festival."

"Good. Then we'll do it. Did you bring your guitar?"

"Oh, yes, but I'm a rank amateur."

Kate laughed. "I didn't mean you had to perform. But I hoped you'd bring it. Peg says you're good."

"Not yet. But I want to be."

"You will. Them that wants gits." She picked up the check. "Shall we go?"

As they drove out of town, Marcie told Kate about Ossipee Joe and about Vin and about the group she played with sometimes at college. It surprised her to hear herself chattering so much. She hoped she wasn't boring Kate. But Kate was listening intently and asking questions.

"I've got a young cousin you'll have to meet. Eric. He's sixteen. He's going to be a classical musician, I guess—clarinet—but he loves to play with jazz groups and sometimes even with friends who play bluegrass. I guess the clarinet is not exactly a bluegrass instrument, but somehow it gets to be when Eric wants it to be."

Marcie felt happy. This trip was going to be a lot more than Peg's wedding, nice though that would be. A music festival! Wow!

# 6

Marcie and Kate took turns driving. It was exciting to Marcie to see the South. She was surprised at how many Souths there were, from the lush Virginia meadows to the Carolina piedmont to the cotton fields of Alabama. In Mississippi they ran into the aftermath of a flash flood and had to drive bumper to bumper through water up to the hubcaps. They saw people in boats piled with household goods. It was the kind of thing Marcie had seen on TV, but this was real. She kept getting that odd sense, over and over, of reality itself seeming somehow eerier, more unreal than the news stories on television. Maybe it was because those were real people in real boats, and the silence of the flooded area with the cabin roofs sticking out of the water seemed more like some other world than the one created by the rapid-fire commentary of reporters as quick pictures came and went before one's eyes.

Kate was an ideal traveling companion, except that she had odd eating habits. Four times a day she would suddenly say "I've got to eat," no matter where they were. They had meals, or at least sandwiches and coffee, in a lot of places that Marcie would just as soon have bypassed; shacky places in the middle of nowhere that sold greasy hamburgers, or some little place on a river that served nothing but catfish. But Kate got nervous and jumpy when she was hungry, so Marcie made no objection.

Every other night she called home, as she had promised. Sometimes her mother wasn't there, so she switched the call to Nana or her father; but when her mother was there, she was full of woe about how lonely she was. Marcie tried to kid her out of it.

"Come on, Mom. You're never home when I call. Your social life must be swinging."

"Well, I have to do something," her mother said. "I can't just sit here and worry."

But her mother seemed far away, and Marcie didn't think about her much. Too many other things demanded her attention. Driving along the gulf was a whole new South, and by the time they reached the long bridge across Lake Pontchartrain, she was almost sick with excitement.

The sky was dark with thunderheads, and the usually placid lake was covered with whitecaps. The car radio mentioned a possible hurricane building up in the Caribbean.

"It's early for hurricanes," Kate said. "Probably it won't come to much. September is the time for the big ones."

"I've never seen a hurricane," Marcie said, "or even a tornado."

Kate grinned. "Cheer up. You probably will someday. Don't feel underprivileged."

The rain came in a torrent just as they reached the far side of the bridge. Kate took the wheel, and Marcie strained to see New Orleans through the downpour. She had a blurred impression of motels and gas stations, and traffic that went too fast. Kate made a quick detour through the French Quarter so she could see the Mississippi, but it was almost invisible in the rain. She got a glimpse of the cathedral and the museum where Kate said there was a death mask of Napoleon.

She made out the French street names and saw the iron grillwork on the restored nineteenth century houses. It looked like what she imagined a European city would look like, a small French city maybe, or a corner of Paris. It was about as far from Marcie's New England village as the moon.

Kate's friends lived in the residential area called Metaire, pronounced, Marcie learned, Met-a-ry. The Paines, Dick and Charlotte, lived in a neat white frame house on a street that had a canal running down the middle of it.

When Kate and Marcie had had time for a shower and a cold drink, Dick told them he wanted to take them to Brennan's for dinner and then across the river to the music festival. At that Marcie completely forgot that she was tired.

Brennan's was in the Quarter. Marcie was so busy absorbing impressions, she felt like a camera. The rain had changed to a fine mist, and now she could see things more clearly. The river astonished her because it seemed higher than the street, and that must surely be impossible. But Dick explained about the levee and took her up some steps so she could get a closer look. Right on cue, a tanker, looking enormous in the rain, came along the river in total silence, like a ghost ship.

"I'm never going home," she said.

"It's supposed to be a good festival," Charlotte said, after dinner as they drove across the Huey Long suspension bridge in the Paines' Honda. "Otherwise we'd have taken you to Bourbon Street for the Dixieland."

"Bourbon Street ain't what it used to be," Dick said.

Marcie had no idea what to expect. They drove into St. John's Parish, into the flat bayou country, until they came to a KOA campground, close to the river. The rain had stopped, and it was nearly dark. A big banner strung across the entrance to the campground said BAYOU COUNTRY AND BLUE-GRASS FESTIVAL. Wooden benches and lawn chairs were scattered randomly around the grounds, and there was a small makeshift stage lit up by lights plastered with insects. Behind everything, the river flowed black and wide and still, with an occasional small island barely visible in the fading light. Near the parking lot a crudely made pirogue was overturned, and some people were sitting on the keel.

People were lined up near a beer keg, waiting with Dixie cups. The sounds of music were everywhere, groups playing in the parking lot and along the river, as well as the group that was playing now on the stage. The dank smell of the river pervaded everything, and mosquitoes attacked like miniature dive bombers.

A bluegrass group called the Crescent City Ramblers was just finishing a set on the tiny stage as Marcie found an empty chair nearby and sat down to listen. For a second the thought flashed through her mind that this was a night when she was supposed to call her mother, but the thought disappeared as quickly as it had come.

She looked around for Kate and the Paines, but she didn't see them; it occurred to her that she should look for them, but the Ramblers went flying into their last number and she forgot everything else.

A new group replaced them, called the Tarheel Six, from North Carolina. Banjo, mandolin, guitar, bass guitar, and two fiddles. The music came at her in a rush of speed that made her scalp tingle. She tried to concentrate on the guitar to see how he got those bass runs and played the rhythm at the same time. Ossipee Joe did something like that.

She watched the way he held his flat pick. Joe had given her a flat pick, but she had used it to pick out quiet leads, not to strum loud like that, clear and distinct over the other instruments. It wasn't flashy, but it made the guitar as important as the other instruments, not just an accompaniment. The complex harmonies and the speed of the instrumentals made her heart thump.

She tore her attention away from the guitar to watch the banjo, the mandolin, and the fiddles when they took their breaks. The fiddles played in harmony with each other. At the end of the number she leaned back feeling wrung out. To be able to play like that!

She stayed to hear the other groups that followed the Tarheel Six. They were all so good she could hardly decide which was best. She felt mind-boggled.

When the last group had finished, and the judges had announced the winners, she looked around, dazed, remembering Kate and the others.

Kate found her. "How'd you like it?"

Marcie shook her head in wonder. "I've never heard anything so good."

"I'm glad we were here for it."

When they got home, Charlotte made coffee, and they sat in the kitchen talking about the concert and then about other things, but Marcie's thoughts stayed with the music. She heard it over and over in her head, wanting to remember some of those breaks. She wished she could get her guitar out of the car and try them, but it was one o'clock in the morning, and anyway she would be too shy to do it in front of other people.

"You look tired," Charlotte said to Kate. "You feeling okay?"

Marcie looked at Kate, ashamed of herself for not having noticed how pale and drawn Kate looked. Her mother was right, she was so self-absorbed, she never noticed how other people were feeling.

"I need a shot and some sleep," Kate said, "and some exercise. I've been sitting ever since we left North Carolina."

"Let's get up early and go swim in the Maguires' pool," Charlotte said. "You remember the Maguires. I have a key to their pool gate."

"Good," Kate said. "I'd like that. Marcie? Want to swim in the morning?"

Marcie grinned. "If I wake up." The fatigue of the long day was suddenly catching up with her, and she couldn't suppress a yawn.

Dick got up, putting his coffee cup in the sink. "The last one in bed is a rotten egg. Putrid!"

As Marcie stretched out in the comfortable guest bed, she remembered Kate's saying she needed "a shot." Of what? She hadn't seen her drink anything except coffee and tea. She had even skipped the light beer that Dick served before dinner, and he had brought her a glass of Perrier. Oh, well. Maybe it was just an expression. Or like a shot of B-12 or something. Before she finished the thought, she was asleep.

# 7

 It was after nine when she woke. The gentle whirr of the overhead ceiling fan was a sound she couldn't place at first. Then she sat up, remembering where she was.

The house was silent. In the kitchen she found a note and a little hand-drawn map showing her where the Maguires' pool was. But the note said, "Back about ten," so she decided to make herself some toast to go with the coffee in the automatic coffee-maker. Another piece of paper with an arrow pointed to a glass-covered dish containing a delicious-looking croissant, that changed her mind about the toast.

With bluegrass still running through her head, she unlocked the car and got her guitar; and while she finished her coffee, she began picking out tunes, getting a chord right, stopping for a swallow of coffee, trying another chord and messing it up, and so on, till she was through with breakfast and ready to go at the music seriously.

She could almost, but not quite, get that break the guitar in the Tarheel Six had used in "Billy in the Low Ground." She tried it over and over and then stopped for another cup of coffee.

She glanced at the kitchen clock and said, "Mom!" She had forgotten to call. She put in a reversed charge call and waited impatiently while the phone at home rang and rang. Maybe Mom was across the street doing aerobics with Fanny Petrelli. Or hanging over the back fence with Mrs. McGraw. Or more likely downtown buying some last-minute things for the wedding; she was always buying clothes and then changing her mind and exchanging them.

Marcie was about to hang up when her mother answered, breathless. "Hello? Hello?"

The operator went through the will-you-accept-the-charges bit, and Marcie said, "Hi, Mom."

"Marcie, thank heaven. I was worried sick."

"I'm sorry. We didn't get in till late . . ."

"What? I can't hear you."

"I said we were out late, and I forgot to call—"

"Honey, you don't have to scream. You're splitting my eardrum."

"Oh, shit," Marcie said under her breath, and of course her mother heard that.

Her tone turned chilly. "Most people have learned by the age of eighteen to use a telephone properly. And not to use vile language. That's a federal offense, in case you don't know."

Marcie took a deep breath. "How are you doing, Mom? Are you all packed?"

"Just about. How is your sister?"

"I have no idea. I'm in New Orleans."

"New what?"

"Orleans. Louisiana. Mom, last night we went to the most wonderful music festival—"

Her mother interrupted. "What are you doing in New Orleans?"

"We're on our way to Austin. The road goes through New Orleans."

"Marcie, this connection is terrible. Why don't you hang up and call back? No, I'll call you back. What's your number? It costs twice as much to call collect, you know. What is your number?"

Marcie saw the Paines' Honda turn into the driveway. "What, Mom? Sorry, we have a lousy connection." Two could play that game. "I'll call you from Austin. Glad you're okay. Love to Nana." She hung up. "Whew," she said to herself and got up to greet Charlotte and Kate, both of them looking rested and relaxed in damp bathing suits.

The two friends spent another half-hour talking over a second cup of coffee while Marcie went outside to explore— and to leave them together so they could talk about whatever old friends who seldom saw each other had to talk about. She had never been away from any of her friends very long. Her best friend Josie went to the same college she did, and Vin came up from the University of Maine fairly often for a weekend in Boston. She saw her other friends when she came home on her frequent visits. I have lived in a tight little circle, she thought. No wonder nothing has ever happened to me.

She walked down the street. It was hot and so humid that the air seemed almost to drip. The canal in the middle of the road smelled faintly evil. What an unhygienic arrangement, she thought. No wonder they had mosquitoes the size of 707's.

But everyone's yard blossomed in a riot of vivid flowers, and the Johnson grass was cut in neat, close-cropped lawns. It was coarser than the grass at home. She picked a blade and felt its sharpness against her finger like a knife prick.

When she got back to the Paines' house, Kate was loading her things into the car. Charlotte hugged Marcie. "Come back to see us," she said, and Marcie felt good, sure that Charlotte meant it.

"I called Manuel," Kate said, as she maneuvered their way out of the city. "He's back from Washington."

Marcie tried to think who Manuel was, but she couldn't remember having heard that name. "Who is Manuel?"

"Oh, sorry. I forget that Peg is not the great communicator. Manuel Garcia. My best fella."

"Oh." Marcie felt a bit dashed. Here she was thinking she had begun to know Kate quite well, and she had known nothing at all about something as important as a best fella. "Tell me about him."

"Well, we met at UT. He was in law school. He does a lot of work for the Civil Liberties Union. He's pretty much into politics. It was Manuel who got John interested in law. In fact, they may end up forming a partnership after John's worked a while with Johnson, Perkins, Friendly, to get his feet wet, so to speak. Manuel is, obviously, a Latino. Pretty damned handsome, if you ask me." She gave Marcie her brilliant grin. "With a lot inside that handsome head. And he cares about people, really cares."

"Will I meet him?"

"You betcha. He's going to be John's best man."

"My sister is a mine of noninformation," Marcie said. "Mostly she scribbles a postcard or calls up. She never told me there was a Manuel."

"Well, there is, but of course there are the obvious problems." Kate looked sad.

Marcie studied her face, trying to figure out what she meant. What obvious problems? She didn't like to ask. Maybe Peg would tell her.

When they got out of the city, Kate asked Marcie to drive, and for a long time Kate sat with her head back against the seat rest and her eyes closed. She looked pale. Marcie wanted to ask if she was all right, but she wasn't sure whether Kate had fallen asleep or not.

Later when it was time for lunch, Kate seemed okay again, so Marcie said nothing. Her mother was forever asking her if she felt all right, and she had come to think of it as an intrusion. It was one of her mother's ways of getting attention.

Marcie was excited when they crossed the Texas state line. She was beginning to feel quite traveled. It amazed her that the United States had so much diversity, and she had only begun to see it.

Texas itself changed. The hilly eastern country was pretty, and then there was Houston, thrusting itself into the sky like a transplanted northern city.

Austin was a total surprise. It was getting dark when they drove into the city limits, Kate now at the wheel. They had agreed that Marcie would spend that night at Kate's apartment and move over to John's family place in the morning. It had been a long drive and both of them were tired.

"Anyway," Kate said, "Peg and John are at our cousin Mabel's party. I was hoping I'd arrive too late for it, and we did." She grinned at Marcie. "I like people one on one. I'm not big on parties. Mabel, by the way, is Eric's mother, he of the clarinet."

The Austin traffic seemed to Marcie to move very fast, but the remarkable thing about the city was the abundance of trees. Kate lived in a small apartment house in the Hyde Park area, a pleasant residential part of the city. A friend who had stayed there while Kate was away had left the refrigerator stocked and clean sheets on the beds. The place was small but attractive, with a big framed print of Winslow Homer's "Woodsman and Fallen Tree" dominating one wall. The furniture was a comfortable mixture of nineteenth century oak and slightly shabby modern. All of it looked used and inviting.

Kate fixed them grilled cheese sandwiches and cocoa, and they headed for bed. The guest room was a small room opening on a patio. There was a picture of a middle-aged couple on the bureau.

"Is that your mom and dad?"

"Yes," Kate said. "They're in England for the summer."

Remembering that Kate had said her mother was her favorite relative, she said, "You must miss them."

"I do, of course, but they're gone a lot. I mean they always have been, since I was old enough. Before that, I tagged along, too. My father is an economist, and he spends a lot of time in foreign universities, lecturing and what-not. I'm an only kid. I'm sort of used to being solitary. I can't imagine what it would be like to have sisters or brothers."

"It's nice," Marcie said, "on the whole. Especially after a certain age."

Later, when she was undressed and had found her tooth-brush in the jumbled contents of her canvas bag, she started for the bathroom.

She stopped short. Kate was in there sitting on the edge of the tub, a syringe in her hand. Marcie stared at her in bewilderment. Kate shooting up? Kate of all people? Heroin? She couldn't believe it. She started to back away.

Kate looked up and saw her. "I'll be out of here in a minute. Maybe you'd give me a hand. I seem to be more inept than usual. Maybe because I'm tired." She was trying to bunch up the flesh of her upper arm. She looked up, when Marcie didn't answer. "Do shots bother you? Some people get kind of sick, even seeing other people. I'm so used to it myself, it's like brushing my teeth. Just one more damned nuisance."

Totally confused, Marcie went into the bathroom. Maybe Kate had allergies or something. It *couldn't* be drugs. Could it?

"If you'd grab hold of my arm, right here, bunch it up so I can get into the muscle . . . Don't be afraid of squeezing." Kate poised the needle over the upper arm. "Tighter, okay? Yeah, good."

Marcie trembled as if the needle had gone into her own flesh. "Is that . . ." she began. "I mean, what *is* that stuff?"

Now it was Kate who looked surprised. "Insulin. I'm diabetic. Didn't you know?" She gathered up the syringe and the vial. "I really ought to do a test, but I'm too tired. Okay, friend, the bathroom is all yours. Sleep well, and don't worry about getting up. I'll probably sleep late myself."

When she was gone, Marcie closed the door and leaned against it. She could see herself in the mirror over the sink. "You dope," she said. "You stupid jumper-to-conclusions." She pulled off her terrycloth robe and stepped into the shower, wishing all her naiveté and her stupid assumptions would

41

wash down the drain. Diabetes. What did that mean? Would Kate die? She leaned against the cool tile wall of the shower and tried to think about it. But it was unthinkable. Surely doctors knew how to deal with things like that nowadays, didn't they? She felt so tired, she could hardly stand up.

John's parents, whom Kate called Aunt Meg and Uncle Joe, lived southwest of the city on a small farm with a large rambling house, a barn, and a corral. A few chickens, pecking around in the gravel near the front door, scattered as the car drove up. The house needed paint, but it looked pleasant and inviting.

Marcie felt nervous. Would they like her? She was so different from her sister. Peg had great charm and outgoingness, but Marcie always felt a little shy with strangers. It was nearly noon, and when Kate stopped the car, she said, "Destination accomplished. Forgive me if I introduce you and then bolt for the refrigerator."

Over breakfast Marcie had asked some questions about

diabetes, and she had learned that Kate had had it all her life, and that the reason she periodically had to eat "right then" was the disease. She had to be careful about exact amounts of the right foods at the right times. Looking back, Marcie remembered the dry-looking cheese sandwiches Kate had consumed sometimes when Marcie was enjoying (or not enjoying, depending on where they had to stop) a hamburger or a pizza.

A tall, spare woman with gray hair was coming toward them from the barn. She wore faded jeans and a plaid cotton shirt and scarred boots.

"Aunt Meg," Kate said.

Marcie was surprised. She knew Aunt Meg was a biology professor at UT, and she had expected an intense, bespectacled, intellectual-looking person.

Kate gave her aunt an enthusiastic hug. "This is Marcie. And after fifteen hundred miles or so, I'm prepared to say she's a sweetie."

Aunt Meg smiled, her tanned face crinkling. She had pale blue eyes. "Fifteen hundred miles is a good test." She hugged Marcie. "Welcome."

Marcie's mother would never had hugged a stranger. Marcie was surprised into exclaiming, "Oh! This is going to be wonderful!"

Kate laughed. "See y'all in the kitchen."

"Come in and cool off," Aunt Meg said. "It's going to be a scorcher. Peg and John will be here any minute. They finally got around to going to pick out a silver pattern. There's nothing like leaving things till the last minute. All the aunts are going crazy because they won't get their presents here before the wedding." She had a soft southern voice.

The house was cool. A wide hall opened into a series of

rooms on each side, the whole shaped like an L with a patio and a small pool in the area between the two arms of the house.

"Your mother called," Aunt Meg said. "She'll be here tomorrow on the five ten from Dallas. I hope she won't be baffled by the Dallas airport. It's so enormous. Here comes Fanny with iced tea. Fanny dear, this is Marcie. Isn't she pretty?"

Fanny was a small, middle-aged woman, who at the moment was carrying a silver tray with a pitcher and glasses. "Peg says you don't look like her, but I see a family resemblance, don't you, Meg?"

"I think so. Stay and have some tea, Fanny."

"I've got to see to the chickens."

"Fanny," Aunt Meg said as Fanny left the room, "is my dearest friend. She's been with us since John was born, and I don't think I could function without her, emotionally as well as practically."

Kate came into the room chewing on a roast chicken leg. "Thanks for the nourishment, Aunt Meg. I've got to buzz off. Manuel awaits."

"Impatiently, I'm sure," Meg said. She held out her left hand to Kate. "How you feeling, love?"

"Right as rain. Just a mite tired, but nothing sleep won't fix." She bent and kissed the top of her aunt's head. "See you anon, Marcie. Oh, and incidentally . . ." she scribbled down a phone number and gave it to Marcie. "Any time you want to get away from the madding crowd, feel free. Just give me a ring."

Marcie walked to the door with her. "Thank you for everything."

"Likewise." Kate hugged her.

"Wait. You don't have a ride home."

"I'm borrowing Uncle Joe's pickup. That'll do fine." She waved and walked away with her quick, swinging walk, toward the barn. A few minutes later she roared down the drive in the old Ford pickup.

"Kate," Marcie said to Aunt Meg, "is wonderful."

"Indeed. They don't come any more wonderful." She looked sad for a moment. "I have a very persistent, demanding prayer in to the Lord for a cure for diabetes, *soon*." She turned toward the other wing of the house. "Fanny has already taken your things to your room, I see. Let me show you where it is and how to find everything. There's a minute pool in the patio, better for cooling off than for lap swimming, but use it whenever you want. Joe says we don't use it enough to make it pay, so he'd be happy to see you splashing around in it."

She took Marcie to a simply furnished room that had a second door opening on the patio. "I'll leave you to your own devices, but make the house your own. You're one of the family."

Marcie was floating on her back in the pool half an hour later when Peg and John came back. Peg let out a whoop and waded into the pool, shorts, T-shirt and all, and hugged her sister. John, tall and thin and bespectacled, waited grinning until Marcie and Peg climbed out, but he hugged Marcie so thoroughly that he was damp, too.

"You look wonderful!" Peg was saying. "You've grown up. My God, John, she's grown up!"

"They do, you know," John said. "How was your trip, Marcie? How's Kate?"

"I'll answer that." It was Kate, in the doorway, with a tall, dark and, Marcie thought, incredibly handsome man just behind her. Kate hugged Peg and John and said to her cousin, "It was a great trip and I feel fine. How about you? You're looking very groomly."

"Feeling groomly. How are you, Manuel, as if I didn't know, having seen you two hours ago. Marcie, this is Manuel Garcia. He's going to be on the Supreme Court someday."

Manuel laughed and shook hands with Marcie. "I've been hearing about you. Don't mind John. He thinks I'm going to make the Supreme Court because I know more than he does about torts."

"Why doesn't everybody come inside and I'll make sherry flips," John said. "I am famous, Marcie, for my sherry flips. I even make a good one for Kate without the sherry. The flipless flip."

He looked like his mother, Marcie thought. She remembered the one time she had seen him, on a very brief visit when Peg had made the obligatory presentation to the family of her future husband. Marcie had expected Robert Redford, but John looked more like a young Buddy Ebsen with glasses. Her mother had said he looked like an undernourished stork, but her mother, of course, had disliked him sight unseen.

"You'd better call Mom," Peg said to her, when she had dressed and joined the others in the living room.

"Why?" She didn't want to go off and spend half an hour on the phone when everyone else was having fun talking and laughing and sherry flipping. She had never heard of a sherry flip, let alone had one.

"Because she called last night, and she told me five times by actual count to be sure you called as soon as you got here, so she'd know you made it safely."

"In spite of being in Kate's clutches," Kate said.

"You'd have thought Marcie was making a trip across the Sahara or something," Peg said to the others.

Marcie felt foolish. Like a child. "I've called her three or four times already. I'll see her tomorrow, for heaven's sake."

"Oh, give the old girl a ring. Why risk a scene?"

It annoyed Marcie that Peg was hassling her to call her mother, Peg who never called her from one month's end to another. She accepted the glass John offered her and sat down. Peg gave her a searching look and shrugged.

"Your funeral," she said.

Marcie bit her tongue and didn't say, "It always has been." She didn't want to feel irritated with her sister. This ought to be a happy time.

John, as if reading her mind, changed the subject and began a funny, dry story about one of the men in the firm he was going to work for.

Manuel told some stories of his own about a Civil Liberties case he was working on in behalf of a Salvadoran family of refugees who were in danger of being deported because they couldn't prove that their lives would be endangered if they went home.

For Marcie it was a new world, all of it; the Texans, the things they were interested in; Manuel's Mexican background; and later, when Uncle Joe joined them, his stories about a graduate class in Economics for High School Teachers that he was teaching during the summer. He was a tall, good-looking man, broad-shouldered and fit, much younger-looking than he must be, Marcie thought.

Having been raised in a family where tension dominated, she looked to see what kind of relationship existed between Meg and Joe, but it was hard to tell. They were courteous to each other, attentive to each other's needs . . . he refilled Meg's glass, she got him his cigar . . . but there was no indication of how they really felt. Marcie was curious. She would ask Peg later.

When Kate and Manuel were leaving, Manuel turned back and said quietly to Marcie, "Thanks for taking good care of my Kate on your trip."

Marcie was surprised and touched. For a moment she couldn't think what to say. "I don't think I took care of her. It was more the other way around."

He smiled. His teeth looked very white against his tan skin, and his eyes were warm. "She likes you."

"Oh, I'm glad. I think she's wonderful."

"You got it." He nodded and turned away to join Kate, who was already in his car. Kate waved.

"What terrific people," Marcie said to Peg. "What a terrific family and bunch of friends you're getting yourself."

Peg smiled. "You betcha." Then she stopped smiling. "If Mom is rude to any of these people, I swear to God I'll throw her out."

"Oh, Peg, come on! At least give her credit for good manners."

"There are ways and ways of being rude," Peg said darkly.

# 9

Impatiently, she watched the people coming down the ramp from the plane. Some of them looked hot and tired, some of them looked eager. None of them looked like a mother from Massachusetts. What if she'd gotten lost in the Dallas airport? Surely everyone was off the plane by now. There came one of the flight attendants, her neat blue jacket slung over her shoulder, her wheeled suitcase trundling along behind her. How did they manage to look so fresh and well-groomed at the end of a flight? She felt hot and rumpled, and all she'd had to do was wait.

Mom would look good, too; she always did. She fussed at Marcie to brush her hair fifty strokes every night, as if that were a magic number; or to paint her fingernails; or press her jeans. Nobody pressed jeans.

Marcie began to worry. What did you do if you lost your mother in the Dallas–Fort Worth airport? Mom should have come with Nana. It had been a bit hard to explain to John's family about that, but Peg had interrupted her attempt at a plausible explanation by saying, "They never do anything together. They can't stand each other." Marcie had been embarrassed, but no one seemed surprised.

Suddenly her mother appeared. She hadn't seen Marcie yet. For a moment Marcie had that same weird sensation, as if she were seeing the other half of herself. It shook her, and she couldn't move.

Her mother looked so small, as if she had shrunk in the last five days. Maybe it was because Marcie had gotten used to the tallness of John's family.

Then her mother saw her. Visible relief swept across her face, and then a look of happiness, as if she were meeting a child she hadn't seen for years. Poor Mom. She really did need people. For a moment Marcie understood in a new and stomach-wrenching way how much her father's abandonment had hurt her mother. She went toward her.

Her mother clung to her for a minute and then stood back to look at her. "I hate planes. The woman next to me kept jabbing me with her elbow. She was so big, she really should have bought two seats."

They walked along the corridor to the baggage claim. "You look great," Marcie said.

"You never called last night. I was worried sick."

"Mom, that's silly."

"What are they like?"

"The Fentons? Oh, they're great. I love them." She gave a glowing description of Meg and John, not so detailed about Uncle Joe, whom she felt she didn't really know.

51

"Well, you always exaggerate. I hope they're going to be all right."

On the drive to the Fentons', her mother filled her in on the local gossip. "I suppose your father isn't here yet?"

"He's coming tonight, and Nana gets in tomorrow morning."

"Mother could have flown with me, but she's so cussedly independent, she has to do everything alone." She leaned forward as Marcie turned into the driveway. "Is that the place? I thought it was a big Texas ranch. Like the one in 'Dallas.' I told Mrs. McGraw it was a ranch like 'Dallas.' "

"Mom, Peg never said anything like that."

"She said ranch. I thought a Texas ranch . . . good heavens, they've got chickens in the front yard! If Mrs. McGraw saw this, I'd never live it down. The house needs painting. Are they poor or what? Look at that terrible grass, like weeds."

"Mother, it's Johnson grass. It's what grows in Texas."

"I'm really surprised."

At that moment Aunt Meg came out of the house, and then Peg, with John at her heels, and finally Fanny in a big white apron.

Marcie's mother put on her most charming smile. "Peg." She hugged her daughter. "You've lost weight."

Peg laughed and exchanged glances with Marcie. "I could stand to, Mom. Here's John."

John held out both hands. "It's great to see you."

"My son-in-law," she said. She looked at Meg. "I've never had a son-in-law before. And you must be John's mother."

Aunt Meg shook hands warmly. "I've never had a daughter either. It feels odd, doesn't it. It's finally dawned on me that I'm the older generation."

52

"Oh, never!" Marcie's mother gave her infectious giggle. "You're only as old as you feel."

Marcie shuddered at the cliché, but she gave her mother marks for trying to be nice. Her mother looked at Fanny, and Marcie hastened to introduce her.

"Ah," her mother said. "An aunt? A cousin? I've heard that Texans number their cousins by the dozens, as Gilbert and Sullivan would say."

"I'm the housekeeper," Fanny said, with her sweet smile.

"And solver of all our problems and our dearest friend," Meg added, putting her arm around Fanny as if, Marcie thought, to protect her from the involuntary look of shock that had been visible for a second on her mother's face. In her mother's world housekeepers didn't greet the guests as one of the family.

But she rallied gallantly. "How nice. I wish I had a friend like that. But I'm so fortunate to have Marcie. I don't know how I would survive without Marcie." She put her hand on her daughter's shoulder.

It was an awkward moment. Marcie felt the tremor in her mother's hand, and she had the same urge to protect her that Meg had felt for Fanny.

Later when her mother was settled in the other guest room, Peg came into Marcie's room. "The old girl hasn't lost her skill at wheeling and dealing, has she," Peg said.

Marcie frowned. "Come on, Peg, give her a break."

Peg shrugged. "We've all been giving her a break all our lives. That's the trouble. She's spoiled rotten."

"You've been giving her breaks?"

Peg flushed. "All right, so I left home. Is that some kind of criminal act?"

"Of course not."

"I know you think I left you holding the bag, but for God's sake, Marcie, don't hold it. You're eighteen. She's a perfectly healthy woman, well provided for. Leave."

"Well, I'm trying to. Give me time. You don't realize how she still suffers over losing Dad . . ."

"But that's her problem, not yours. Oh hell, let's don't fight over Mom. You want to go with me in the morning when I pick up Nana?"

"Sure. What about Dad?"

"He's getting in late tonight. He said he'd go straight to the Driskill. We'll all get together for breakfast after Nana gets in." She hesitated. "Dad wants us to have breakfast with him. I mean all of the family, before all the togetherness gets underway. He invited John, but John thinks he'd be butting in. He thinks he's not family yet."

"You mean Mom, too?"

"Yeah. I haven't broken it to her yet."

"Oh. I don't think she'll do it."

"Well, all we can do is try. Back me up, will you?"

Marcie sighed. "All right. It won't be exactly a joyous feast."

# 10

"I had no idea," Nana said, "that Texas was so pretty."

"It isn't," Peg said. "At least not all of it. Austin and the hill country around here are unusually nice. Stick around till I get back from the honeymoon and I'll show you Fredericksburg and the LBJ ranch and a lot of nice places."

"You tempt me," Nana said. She was hanging up her things in the hotel closet. "I like this hotel very much. It's old, isn't it?"

"Yes. And you're right on Sixth Street. On Saturday night you can cruise the street with all the types. Have a beer at Maggie Mae's, catch Ferron's concert at the Ritz, window-shop at Bookwomen, and say no, thank you, to the drug dealers."

55

"Don't think she won't," Marcie said. "Cruise, I mean."

"When in Rome," Nana said. "Is your mother all right?"

"You sound as if she's recuperating from an illness," Peg said.

"She's been recuperating for four years," Nana said, a little sadly.

"Marcie thinks we're too hard on her."

"We are." Nana sat on the bed and bounced. "Good bed. Yes, we are too hard on her. Marian never really grew up, and it's probably my fault. I don't know how you teach someone at her age to face reality. All I know is, Marcie shouldn't be her cushion."

"Why don't you stay in Austin?" Peg said to Marcie. "You'd love it. There's so much music here, and I'm here, and we could have a ball."

It was so much what Marcie wanted to do, she couldn't bear just then to talk about it. "I'm going to see Dad. Knock on his door after you pick up Mom, okay?" And she fled.

Her father opened the door of his room on the next floor and hugged Marcie. He was still in shirtsleeves, struggling with his tie.

She tied it for him. "You never could tie it straight." She was glad to see him. He never seemed to change. There were no lines in his boyish face, no gray in his thick brown hair. His eyes were like hers. It hurt her when Peg used to say it had always been Peg and Dad versus Mom and Marcie. Marcie loved her father, too; she had seemed to be on her mother's side, perhaps, because Mom needed somebody to stick up for her. "How's Ellen?"

"Great." His face lit up. "Sends her love. It's the first time we've been apart for more than a day since we got married."

Marcie didn't know what to say. She liked her father's wife, but she never felt quite comfortable with her, perhaps because to be friends with her seemed disloyal to her mother.

"I'm glad your mother agreed to come to breakfast. I thought we ought to have a little time together, all of us, before Peg goes zooming off in another direction."

"Peg zoomed off long ago." She wanted to say, "So did you."

"Hey, this is a great town. Did you bring your guitar?"

"Sure."

"I couldn't sleep last night, so I wandered around town. What music! In little bars and dives all over town. If you're going to take a year off from college, which I admit startled me at first till I got to thinking how much I'd like to have done the very same thing at your age—I mean just grab my banjo and take off . . . Anyway if you're going to do that, why not do it here? Peg would be here, and you could—"

Marcie interrupted him. "What about Mom?" She knew the question would make him feel guilty, and she saw in his face that it did.

"Marcie, you've got to live your own life. Your mother has to grow up."

"I'm sick of hearing that," she said. "It isn't any answer."

He turned away, looking hurt, and put on the jacket of his linen suit.

"I'm sorry," she said. "I'm feeling badgered right now."

"Sorry. I didn't mean to badger." He sounded stiff. "But whatever you do, I'll foot the bill, within reason." He began to loosen up. He never could stay angry long with his children. "Maybe Ellen and I could come down for a visit this winter. Soak up some sunshine and hear some music."

"I don't think this is exactly the sunbelt."

"Well, it beats Massachusetts." He started at the knock on the door. "That must be Marian and Peg . . ." He was suddenly nervous. "Is my tie okay?"

Touched, she adjusted his tie and kissed his cheek. "You're fine, Pop. And thanks for the offer."

It was Peg at the door. "Mom and Nana are already downstairs in the dining room," she said. "Everybody's just a tad nervous, Pop." She hugged him.

"Me too," he said. "Maybe it wasn't such a great idea. Listen, I could just slip off, and you guys could . . . you know, put it on my bill . . ."

"Oh, no, you don't." Peg put her arm through his. "You thought of it, you're stuck with it."

"It'll be okay, Dad," Marcie said. But she was nervous, too.

Most of the meal went well because each of them worked so hard at it. Nana and her son-in-law, who were obviously fond of each other, regaled the others with travel stories. He was careful not to mention Ellen when he talked about his visit to Japan, and Nana came through at once with stories of Red China and Hong Kong. Marcie's mother chattered, commented, laughed a little shrilly, sometimes in the wrong places, and Marcie and Peg prompted when prompting was needed. Later, Marcie couldn't remember a thing she had eaten.

Just at the end of the meal, however, Marcie's father turned to his ex-wife and said, "Marian, in case we don't get a chance to chat again before I leave, I want to make a suggestion."

She looked at him suspiciously. "Yes?"

"Yeah." He ran his finger around under the front of his collar, and Marcie began to get nervous. He did that when he was getting into something he wasn't sure he could handle. "I was thinking, since Marcie wants a year off to kind of get herself together and explore the music possibilities, Austin seems like a great place for her to spend the year. Peg will be here, and the music is—"

His former wife interrupted him with ice in her voice. "How like you, Tom, to think of something absolutely preposterous and to spring it on us at a time like this."

"What a minute," Peg said, but neither of her parents paid the least attention.

Tom flushed and said, "There's nothing preposterous about it. I'll support her for a year, because I think it's a good idea. And I think she should get clear away from home."

Marian's voice grew more shrill, and Peg glanced around quickly to see if they were being overheard. Marcie was clutching her coffee cup as if her life depended on it. "I have agreed to her year off, as you call it. I have no objection whatever. I do not agree to her getting 'clear away from home.' I'm surprised you haven't suggested she come live with you. You've always tried to take away everything I valued."

"Look here," he said angrily.

"Stop it!" Marcie's voice was low, but they all looked at her. She put down her cup of coffee so hard that it clattered in the saucer and some of the coffee spilled on the tablecloth. "I am not a child, and I am not a commodity. *I'll* decide what I'm going to do." She pushed her chair back and headed for the door. Her father started to get up, but Nana put a restraining hand on his arm.

Marcie almost ran through the lobby onto the street. She didn't look where she was going, just started to walk, fast. After the air conditioning of the hotel, the atmosphere was intensely hot and almost liquid with humidity, but she didn't notice. She walked past shops and hotels and people, seeing none of them.

She walked for a long time, until suddenly she was exhausted. Expending that much energy had used up some of her anger, but there was plenty left. She was angry with both of her parents. It was all very well to say her father meant well and that her mother was afraid of losing her, but she was not ready yet to see their point of view. She felt like a football tossed back and forth, each of them trying to make points.

When she went back to the hotel, they had all left except Nana, who was sitting on her bed biting her lip in concentration as she applied nail polish.

"Where are they all?" Marcie flopped into a chair. She was tired, and her feet hurt.

"They went to John's house. Your father hasn't met the Fentons yet."

"Neither have you."

"I will. Damn!" she said as the nail polish brush slipped. Carefully she wiped off the surplus polish with a Kleenex.

"You didn't have to wait for me."

"Honey, I was not waiting for you. An old college chum of mine is going to call. She lives here."

"Oh." Marcie watched her grandmother for a minute. "I'm sorry I pulled a temper tantrum. At least I guess I'm sorry."

"What's to be sorry for? You said what you had a perfect right to say, in a controlled tone of voice, and aside from a small coffee stain on the tablecloth, there was no evidence of temper."

"Except that I stalked off."

"Marcie." Her grandmother put down the bottle of polish. "You had a perfect right. Stop feeling guilty about everything."

"Well, but I ruined Dad's family breakfast."

"Your father is a sweet, well-intentioned man, but he will never make the diplomatic corps. To tell you the truth, I was proud of you."

Marcie looked at her in surprise. "You were?"

"Yes. It's high time you stood up for yourself. You're at an age when you, just you, have to decide what direction your life will take. You are not your mother's keeper nor your father's bad conscience nor your sister's surrogate. You are Marcie. *Be* Marcie, and stop worrying about it."

The phone rang, and Nana's face lit up. "Oh, I hope that's Bridget. I haven't seen her for thirteen years. Can you believe it?" She lifted the phone. "Hello? . . . Bridget!" Her voice rose in a squeal of delight. "Oh, it's good to hear your wonderful croaky Texas voice. How are you, sweetie? I can't wait to see you."

Marcie quietly left the room. She wanted to think awhile before she rejoined the family.

# 11

When Marcie got to the Fentons' house, the first person she saw was her mother. "Mom," she said, "I'm sorry about wrecking breakfast."

"Oh, that's all right, honey. We're all uptight just now. Have you heard the latest?"

"What latest?"

"The maid of honor is in the hospital."

Alarmed, Marcie said, "Kate?"

"Kate. Peg is in a state. She's talking of postponing the wedding, but everybody's trying to talk her out of it."

Marcie tried not to think that her mother seemed pleased. "Is it the diabetes? Is it bad?"

"Diabetic coma." Her mother assumed the solemn look she

used for church and concerts where classical music was played. "It happens now and then, I understand."

Marcie brushed past her and ran into the house. Peg and Aunt Meg and John were standing together, talking, in the living room. Peg's face had traces of tears.

"Peg, is it bad?"

Peg shook her head, her eyes filling with tears again, and Aunt Meg answered. "She's out of the coma. Manuel just called from the hospital. The doctor is optimistic." Her face looked drawn. "But every time it happens . . ." She shook her head.

"She's insisting we go ahead with the wedding," John said. "It's up to Peg."

Marcie's mother joined them. "If you ask me," she began.

"Please, Mother," Peg said. "Nobody did. Not just now."

Offended, her mother left the room.

"Don't be hard on her, dear," Aunt Meg said gently. She put her arm around Peg.

"I can't help it. She never liked Kate. I just don't feel like hearing anything she has to say."

"Let's take a walk," John said to Peg. The two left the room.

Aunt Meg sat down with a sigh. She looked hot and dishevelled. "Poor Kate, I know how she's feeling. So scared she's spoiling the wedding. I really think they should go ahead."

"Could I send her some flowers or something?" Marcie said. She felt like crying herself. Nice, thoughtful Kate.

Aunt Meg shook her head. "She hates to have us treat her like an invalid. She refuses to be one, as much as she can. So we try not to make much of it when she has an attack."

Marcie sat down. "Is it going to . . . to kill her someday?"

Aunt Meg didn't answer for a moment. "The prognosis, as

the doctors like to say, is not good for anyone who has had lifelong diabetes. One of the problems she's struggling with now is whether to marry Manuel or not. Whether it would be better to grab what time they can, or whether it would be too hard on him. Manuel, of course, is more than willing to risk it. He's a lovely man, that Manuel. I think they should get married, myself, but Kate has to decide." She leaned her head back against the chair. "Life does seem unfair at times. But I guess nobody ever claimed it was fair."

She got up abruptly. "There's so much to do."

"Can I help?"

Aunt Meg looked at her distractedly for a moment. "I can't think. I feel disorganized all of a sudden. I guess when Peg comes back, the best thing you could do would be to give her some moral support. You love Kate too and that will help her."

Marcie went to her room, closed the door, and lay down on her bed. She was thinking she ought to listen to people a lot more. "I've been so damned self-centered," she said aloud.

She recognized her mother's knock and tried to pretend she was asleep, but that had never stopped her mother when she wanted to talk.

"I hope I'm not disturbing you," she said, plumping down on the side of Marcie's bed. "I'll be so glad when all this is over. So much emotion all over the place. I've always heard southerners were volatile—" She stopped and peered at Marcie. "Are those tears? Whatever is the matter, honey? Listen, if you're still feeling bad about breakfast, forget it. Your father asked for it. It was a stupid idea in the first place . . ."

"I wasn't thinking of that."

"Then what in the world. . . ?"

"I was thinking about Kate."

"Listen, dear, there's nothing to cry about. You know Mildred Armbruster, she's had diabetes for years. Every now and then she has to pop into the hospital and get shots or something, but diabetes is a perfectly manageable disease these days. It's like polio. I mean who worries about polio any more? When I was growing up—"

"Mother, please. Could you leave me alone for a while?"

Her mother drew back, looking grieved. "Well. I guess I can take a hint." She stood up. "Two days you've been here, and already they've made you hostile to me. Your father's got his heart set on turning you against me, and he'll stop at nothing—"

"Mom, shut up!" At the look on her mother's face, she said, "I'm sorry. But please, leave me alone, okay?"

"Certainly," her mother said, in a voice of ice. She left the room, slamming the door.

# 12

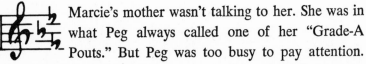 Marcie's mother wasn't talking to her. She was in what Peg always called one of her "Grade-A Pouts." But Peg was too busy to pay attention. The wedding was going forward as planned, and everyone seemed to have something urgent to do. Except Marcie. She had offered, had been thanked, but no chore had been as-assigned. Feeling useless, she put on her swimsuit and went out to the pool. For about twenty minutes she swam hard, and it made her feel a lot better.

In a field near the pool area a goat hung his head over the fence and stared at her with knowing yellow eyes.

She pulled herself out of the pool and sat on the edge with her feet dangling in the cool water. She was wondering what it felt like to be about to get married. Was Peg thinking one in three marriages end in divorce? Probably about-to-be-weds always thought they'd be the lucky ones. Her mother had certainly believed that her marriage was an unchangeable fact, written in the stars, as she liked to say. Poor Mom. Exasperating Mom.

She looked up and saw the goat studying her. "Hello," she said. "What are you thinking about?"

A voice behind her said, "I was thinking I'd flop around in the pool a bit."

She jumped and turned around. A tall, skinny boy, about fifteen or sixteen, stood behind her in faded swim trunks.

"Hi," he said. "I'm Eric. I hope I'm not interrupting any deep conversation with the goat. She's called Mehitabel, in case you didn't know. In case you cared."

"Eric. You're the musician."

"Hope to be." He came and flopped down beside her. "You're Marcie."

"Right."

"You play guitar, right?"

"Right."

"Peg says you're good."

"I guess the answer is, compared to what?"

He shook his head and his dark hair fell in his eyes. "Don't worry about that. I don't. I play clarinet. You like bluegrass, right?"

Marcie grinned. Something about this unsmiling boy made her feel more cheerful. "If I say 'right' again, I'm going to sound like a broken record. I like bluegrass, yes."

"Kate told me. She's feeling better. I came over to tell everybody, but nobody's here. She just has to rest and all that hospital crap for a few days."

"I'm so glad. I really like Kate."

"Yeah, everybody does. She's one of those people. Manuel was going to pick you up for the wedding, but I told him I'd bring you, I hope that's okay. He's so nervous about being best man, he'd probably forget to come for you anyway."

"That's fine."

"Maybe you and me and some friends of mine can get together and whap out some music while you're here." He stood up, lifted his arms, and dove into the pool with a great splash.

Marcie watched him swim for a few minutes, and then she waved and went inside. There was going to be a wedding rehearsal late in the afternoon and then a dinner at a restaurant up in the hills. The wedding was at four the next day. She hoped her mother's mood would improve and that her father wouldn't drink too much at the reception. Sometimes he got carried away. She also hoped her mother wouldn't make any more cracks to Peg about her not getting married at home, "in the proper way." Much more of that, and Peg would start yelling. Her boiling point with Mom was very low.

After the wedding and reception, Marcie intended to have a talk with her mother. In the time she had had, while the wedding work went on, she'd been able to make some plans. Now, she had to tell her mother that she wanted to stay in Austin for a little while; maybe not for the whole year, but at least for a few weeks. Then, but this part she wouldn't say, if she liked it, maybe Mom would have gotten used to not having her around, and she could stay longer. Play it by ear.

# 13

Marcie dressed carefully for the wedding. Peg had bought the gowns for Kate and her. She wondered if Kate would ever get to wear hers. They were really too fancy for anything but a wedding. Marcie's was pale lavendar, long, with a full skirt that had one ruffle at the bottom. The bodice fitted tightly and was simple, with a low v-neck and cap sleeves. It made her feel like a nineteenth-century belle. What a nuisance it must have been to swish around in long skirts; and hoopskirts must have been enough to warp a woman's psyche, not to mention her behind. Nana had one of those frames, which had belonged to her grandmother. She kept saying she should give it to the Peabody Museum or the Essex Institute or some museum. "Only who'd want the dusty old thing?" she always said. "A personal torture chamber, that's what it was."

Marcie was feeling excited. She had never been a bridesmaid. Once she had stood up with friends at the court house, but that didn't count.

The rehearsal had gone well, and the dinner had been a great success. Her mother had played mother-of-the-bride to the hilt, which got her a lot of attention, so she was in a good mood, although she still kept saying she couldn't understand half of what Texans were saying. When Peg said, "Mother, they may have trouble with your accent, too," she had looked astonished and said, "Accent? I don't have any accent." Everyone had laughed indulgently, because actually Mom sounded like the quintessential Yankee, with her broad A's and skipped R's.

Well, Marcie thought, we all have a New England accent, I guess, though Peg's seemed to have diminished. She leaned toward the mirror, applying eye makeup carefully. Cars had been coming and going, but now the house seemed quiet. She knew her mother had gone with Aunt Meg. She'd better get finished and go see if Eric had come. Aunt Meg said he drove what she called a "venerable Chevrolet of uncertain temperament," but Marcie wasn't daunted by that. Most of her friends drove old cars, and she had too until her dad gave her the Escort.

She took one last look at herself in the mirror. It was surprising how different one looked in different clothes. She looked older—almost, she thought hopefully, sophisticated. But nobody would be looking at her, and that was fine with her. If she did anything stupid, they wouldn't notice. Unless of course she tripped and fell on her face going down the aisle.

Eric was in the living room with another young man, older than he was, possibly about Marcie's age. Eric too looked different in his suit and tie. The other man was rather short, good looking, with reddish hair cut very short and brown eyes with glints of red in them. He was in cut-offs and a stained T-shirt.

"I hope I didn't keep you waiting," Marcie said to Eric.

"Just got here. This is Abner Frothingham. My car broke down again. Abner's going to run us over to the church."

"That's nice of him." Marcie smiled at Abner Frothingham.

"The back of your dress isn't zipped all the way up," Abner said. He wiped his hands on his cutoffs and zipped it for her.

"Wow," she said. "Thanks! I should have known I'd get something wrong. Is everything else okay?" For some odd reason she felt at home with this fellow called Abner Frothingham, though it was not usual for her to feel easy with a stranger.

"Perfect." He grinned. "A-okay."

"Abner plays a crazy banjo," Eric said.

She noticed that Abner's T-shirt said MUSIC MOVES MOUNTAINS. "Great." Another fellow-musician. That was why she felt as if she knew him. Good vibes.

"We'd better get started," Eric said. "Ab will take you first, and then come back for me."

Marcie followed them out of the house. Why did he have to take one at a time? Maybe he had a two-seater sports car, and they were being thoughtful about not crushing her dress.

But there was no car in the drive. Abner moved away and came back wheeling a huge, shiny BMW motorcycle. "How do you like 'er?" he said proudly. "I worked all summer for this baby. Cost me fourteen thousand clams. Twenty three more payments and she's all mine."

"It's beautiful," Marcie said, and it was. But in a bridal gown?

Abner beamed and handed her one of the crash helmets that hung from the handlebars. She groaned inwardly, thinking of how long it had taken her to get her hair just right. She took a deep breath and climbed onto the pillion seat, clutching her beaded purse (which, thank God, had a small comb in it) with one hand and Abner with the other. She glanced at Eric, who was watching her with what seemed to be approval.

"Hold tight," Abner yelled, revving the motor.

Eric cupped his mouth with his hands. "Happy landings."

# 14

Abner brought the motorcycle to a fast skidding stop in front of the small church. People were standing around in groups chatting. Marcie's mother, who was talking animatedly to several people, stopped in mid-sentence and stared at Marcie in shock. She came toward her as Marcie climbed off the BMW and Abner sped away. She looked distraught.

"What's the matter?" Marcie said, lamely.

"Your own sister's wedding, and you arrive on a motorcycle with some hippy. Your dress is ruined. I can't believe it."

Marcie looked down at her dress. "It's just a little mussed. And maybe dusty. It'll be all right."

"The groom and the best man are back there eating *apples,* and Peg is *with* them. The priest can't be more than twenty-five years old. I've never seen such an improper wedding."

"Take it easy, Mom. You're suffering from battle fatigue."

Her father came up to them, smiling a little too broadly, obviously not sure whether he was still in his ex-wife's bad graces or not. "Hi, Marian. You look great. Marcie, honey, what are you doing in that crash helmet?"

"Oh, lord, I forgot." She pulled it off. "It's Abner's."

"She came," her mother said, "on a *motorcycle.*"

Marcie's father laughed. "What a great idea. What kind?"

"A BMW. It's gorgeous, Dad." She knew her father longed for a motorcycle of his own.

"I've been looking at 'em. Aren't they something? Boy, motorcycles today are really the state of the art."

Marcie's mother looked at them in disbelief and walked away.

"Poor Mom," Marcie said, and thought how often she had said or thought that lately.

"Marian has trouble with the world," her father said. "You'd better go comb your hair."

She found Peg, who grabbed her and said, "God, I'm glad you're here. Somebody said you were coming with Eric, and that car of his is . . . what are you doing with a crash helmet?"

"Eric's car broke down. Abner Frothingham brought me on his motorcycle."

Peg laughed. "Good for Abner. You'd better comb your hair. God, I'm nervous. Look at John and Manuel, eating Father Steve's apples as if they were on a picnic. I could kill them." But she looked toward John with more love than Marcie had ever seen on her face.

74

She and Peg went into Father Steve's study to wait for the wedding to start.

"Mom thinks we're doing everything wrong. She was supposed to arrive last with Aunt Meg and make a grand entrance, but Aunt Meg's already in the church making sure the flowers are okay. Are we doing everything wrong?"

"How do I know?" Marcie was trying to do something with her hair, standing on tiptoe to see into the priest's tiny mirror high on the wall. "I've never paid much attention to weddings. And I don't suppose anyone here cares very much about all that except Mom." She turned to Peg. "Listen. Have a terrific marriage."

Peg's laugh broke, and her eyes filled with tears. "I'm scared spitless. But I love him. What else is there to do?"

"You know what Nana always says: nothing ventured, nothing gained." She put her arms around her sister. "It's going to be great. John is a sweetheart. Really."

"I know, damn him." Peg laughed and wiped her eyes.

John stuck his head in the door and did a double take. "You're crying! Peg, what's wrong?" His long face tensed into worry lines. "Is it Kate?"

"No. Kate made me promise not to mind that she isn't here. It's just . . . brides always cry."

He looked at Marcie. "Is that right?"

"Sure," Marcie said ."Everybody knows that." She went to him and hugged him. "Stop worrying. Everybody loves you. You've got apple juice on your chin."

He mopped his chin with his handkerchief. "Wonderful apples. Steve's going to give us a bushel when we get back, Peg. Can you make apple pie?"

"No. Can you?"

His face relaxed in a grin. "Yes, as a matter of fact."

Father Steve's boyish face appeared in the doorway. "Everybody on stage. Places, please." He did indeed look not much more than twenty-five.

Downstairs, the organist had begun to play.

"Oh my God," Peg said, "what am I getting into?"

Father Steve laughed. "The classic bride. Get around to the front door. Marcie, where's your bouquet?"

"Oh, no!" Peg wailed. "It's still in Aunt Meg's refrigerator!"

But when they got to the entrance of the church, Aunt Meg was there with Marcie's bouquet. It still felt cold from the refrigerator. "Abner to the rescue again," she said. "Just in the nick."

Marcie heard the BMW roaring off down the street.

"Here we go," said Manuel. "I'm clutching the ring. If I drop it, we'll fake it."

The organ music rose.

"You're on, Marcie," Aunt Meg said. She herself hurried into the church.

Marcie had meant to look at everything, take in all the impressions, but she saw nothing except the flagstones under her feet. They were slightly uneven, and she was terrified of tripping. Her hands trembled so, she thought she would drop the bouquet. The only faces she saw were Aunt Meg's, beaming, with tears in her eyes, and Nana's, smiling encouragingly.

During the ceremony she kept wanting to cry, but she concentrated on staring at Manuel and then at her father, who looked uncharacteristically solemn as he gave away the bride. She didn't hear a word that Father Steve said.

And then it was over. Her sister Peg was somebody new.

# 15

The reception was at a small, attractive country club in the hills. A caterer had done a good job. The long table, spread with platters of small sandwiches, slices of cold duck, paper-thin ham, relishes, and fruit, was inviting. Mom ought to approve of this, at least, Marcie thought.

Her mother was greeting guests, who were saying, "Lovely wedding," "Charming wedding," and so on, and she was being charming herself, saying with an indulgent smile, "Thank you, thank you, not exactly traditional, but young people today . . ." As if young people today were her greatest joy in life.

But when she had a moment alone with Marcie, she said, "This is terrible."

Marcie was startled. "What's terrible?"

"No receiving line. No bride and groom! Where in heaven's name are they?"

"They went directly to the hospital to see Kate. They'll be here in a little while. Does it matter?"

"Of course it matters. It's *inappropriate*." She turned away with a welcoming smile to greet Eric's mother and father and Eric himself, looking slightly uncomfortable.

It struck Marcie that her mother's concern was real. She wasn't trying to be difficult; she really was upset about things not being what she thought of as correct. With Mom, Marcie realized, it's not cleanliess that's next to godliness, it's appropriateness. She found that idea so illuminating, she tracked down Nana to tell it to her.

"Exactly," Nana said. "To be socially improper is somehow to be sinful. How did a child of mine ever get such an idea? Honey, try those wonderful little asparagus sandwiches. And the guacomole dip is fantastic. I wonder if I can get the recipe."

"Have you had any punch?" It was Eric holding out a glass to her. "Hey, you did good. Didn't even trip. But how can people stand it to get married? Even nice people like John and Peg. Boy, I hope they make it."

"Don't be so gloomy. Why shouldn't they?"

"Well, who does? I mean look at your parents. Look at Aunt Meg and Uncle Joe. Look at practically everybody you know—"

Marcie stopped him. "Aunt Meg and Uncle Joe! What do you mean?"

He looked disconcerted. "Oh, well, I . . . Hey, here comes the bride!"

There was a flurry of welcome at the other end of the room, as Peg and John and Manuel came in. Marcie's mother instantly moved to the scene of action, and Marcie heard her clear voice saying to someone, "Yes, I'm the mother of the bride."

Marcie's father brought Marcie a glass of punch. "I've got one," she said.

"Have another. Your mother may not have made it to Hollywood, but by God, she learned to project."

Suddenly irritated, Marcie said, "Cut it out, Dad. I'm sick of hearing everybody knock Mom."

He looked contrite. "I'm sorry, honey. I guess it is kind of crass. Damn good punch, isn't it?"

"But not exactly inocuous." She put her second glass on the table, and he picked it up and drank it. "Take it easy, Pop."

Now it was he who looked irritated. "Don't patronize me, sweetie."

Marcie felt like going home. Parties were not her scene. She liked people one-on-one, or maybe two or three at the most. She went to find Eric, who had wandered off. "I still have Abner's crash helmet," she said. "In my car."

"Where was your car when Abner took you to church?"

"My father borrowed it, to pick up Nana and, I don't know, a couple of John's relatives somewhere. Why?"

"Nothing. The logistics of something like a wedding are fascinating. Are you enjoying this?"

"No."

"Why don't we split? We can go to Ab's place and return the helmet. I think Freddie Ayers is over there. We'll take my clarinet and your guitar and blow ourselves away."

"I think I ought to hang around till Peg and John leave. After that, I'd love to."

"Okay." He refilled both their glasses. "Neat punch."

"Watch it, my boy-o," said Manuel, joining them. "It's lethal."

"How is Kate?" Marcie said.

"Looking more like herself. She got a kick out of seeing the newlyweds." He grinned. "And me in my disguise. She said I look like a respectable WASP with a sunlamp."

Marcie laughed. She liked Manuel. "When is she coming home?"

"Four or five days. Which reminds me." He went through his pockets and found a key. "This is to her apartment. She thought you might want a place to flop for a while. She hopes you won't leave before she gets home."

Marcie was touched. "What a nice thing to do." It solved the problem of where to stay while she made up her mind how long to stay. She wrote down Kate's address on a paper napkin. She was pretty sure she remembered how to get there, but she didn't know the street number.

Aunt Meg came and talked to them for a few minutes. She looked tired. Marcie remembered what Eric had said and wondered what it meant. Probably nothing, she thought, especially when Uncle Joe joined them, refilled their glasses and offered a toast to the newlyweds, his arm around Aunt Meg's shoulders.

A little later, she was aware of her mother at her side, saying, "Marcie, I think you've had enough punch." And Nana saying, "Let the child alone, Marian. It's an emotional day for her." Was it? Marcie wondered. It seemed to her that all days were emotional lately.

A moment later her mother said something to Nana that Marcie didn't catch. Nana turned away, and her mother repeated it, adding, to a woman near her, "My mother is marvelous, but she's getting a little hard of hearing. I guess it comes to all of us."

Marcie heard herself saying, a little too loudly, "Nana is not hard of hearing." She spaced the words, speaking them very distinctly.

Her mother looked startled. "Marcie, I think you . . . really, dear, I think . . ."

But Nana had Marcie by the arm and was leading her away. "Maybe your mother is right," she said. "Ease up on the punch, sweetheart. That's not an order; it's advice."

"Am I drunk or something?" Marcie said.

"Not yet."

Peg came up to them. "We're about to leave," she said. "Marcie, hang around till we get back at least. Two weeks isn't long. Darlin' Nana . . ." She hugged her grandmother. "Are you going to rush off home?"

"Certainly not. My friend and I have wild and wonderful plans."

"Wonderful." Peg kissed them both. Her eyes were shining.

"Happy honeymoon," Marcie said. She wished she were going to the Caribbean on a honeymoon. Only she didn't know anybody she wanted to go with.

In a few minutes they were gone in a shower of rice, a couple of tin cans clanking, and streamers flowing from the car.

Marcie felt let down. People ought to go home now, but they were still eating and drinking and talking as if they were at a party.

"Now?" Eric said, appearing at her side in his sudden way.

"Now," she said, "definitely." She was concentrating on clutching the small, silly beaded purse that she'd carried at the wedding. It had Kate's key in it. "Wait, I have to get my car keys from Dad."

She found her father exchanging apparently uproarious jokes with Uncle Joe and a couple of other men. They stopped so abruptly, she knew they must be dirty jokes. "I need my car keys, Dad."

"Car keys. Right you are." He dug them out of a pocket. "Taking off, honey?"

"For a while. When are you leaving?"

He looked at his Seiko watch. "In about an hour."

"Oh!" She had forgotten it was so soon. "Maybe I should take you to the airport."

" 'Course not. I can take a cab."

"I'll take him," Uncle Joe said. "Not to worry."

Her father took a folded piece of paper out of his pocket and put it in her little purse. "Listen, sweetheart, stick around. This is a good town. Remember what I told you."

She kissed him. "Thanks, Pop. Have a good trip."

She saw her mother staring at her across the long room as she and Eric started out, but she just waved and kept going. Outside in the warm night air, she suddenly realized that maybe she had had too much to drink after all. "Will you drive?" she said.

"Sure. Are you smashed?"

"I don't know."

"That stuff sneaks up on you. Whatever you do, don't drink a lot of water. That'll give you another drunk all over again."

"I don't approve of getting drunk," she said. And they both laughed.

He drove past the Fentons' house and got her guitar, then went to his house for his clarinet. Marcie was half asleep, feeling the motion of the car and its stops and starts. After a while, when he said, "Here we are," she opened her eyes and sat up. The world spun.

"Wow," she said. "Eric, I can see two of you."

He came around to her side of the car. "Take it easy. You can lie down if you want to. Nobody'll hassle you here."

She didn't remember getting into the apartment house and up the stairs. Through a blur she saw Abner and another man with a beard, a big man. She heard Eric say, "Freddie, this is Marcie, but not at the moment. She's had a tad too much wedding punch."

Marcie swayed, but somebody caught her and laid her on a couch that smelled faintly of marijuana and beer. It was good to lie still. Nobody seemed to expect anything of her.

It seemed like a long time later that she was conscious of music. Wonderful bluegrass music. Different from any she had heard before. And finally she made out that it was a clarinet. Whoever heard of bluegrass with a clarinet? She liked it, though. She opened her eyes. The room tilted, whirled, and then steadied. She decided it would be wise not to move for a few minutes. Meanwhile, lie still and listen to that amazing guitar. Who was playing it?

She made an effort to focus on the group at the other end of the room. They were absorbed, quite unconscious of her. It was Eric with the clarinet of course. Abner was playing banjo; and the big man, Freddie, was playing the astonishing guitar. He was fantastic!

When they soared to a finish, she sat up and said, "Wow! What was that?"

They turned to look at her as if they had forgotten she was there.

"Feeling better?" Eric said.

"I think so. Yes. What were you playing?"

" 'Bill Cheatham,' " Abner said. "How was the wedding?"

"Okay, I guess." She looked at the big man. "Are you Freddie?"

"In person." He didn't smile, but his eyes smiled.

"You guys are wonderful. If I could play the guitar like that, I'd die of joy."

"'That'd be too bad." This time he grinned.

"What kind of guitar is that?"

"It's an old Martin."

"Mine is a cheap Yamaha."

"Well, you have to start somewhere."

"One more blast before we break up?" Abner said. "Want to sit in, Marcie?"

"No. I'm not up to it." They thought she meant the way she felt, but she meant her playing wasn't up to it. She listened in awe as they whirled through "John Hardy."

When she could manage to speak, she said to Freddie, "Do you ever give lessons?"

He looked at her for a moment. "Now and then."

Abner picked up Marcie's guitar and handed it to her. "Just whip through a couple bars. Convince him you know one chord from another."

Marcie was scared. She felt as if her whole life depended on playing a few bars well enough. She had never wanted anything so much as she wanted to take lessons from Freddie Ayers. "I'm not really very good . . ." she began.

"Play," Abner said.

All the music she knew seemed to have fled from her mind, so she decided to do the opening of "John Hardy," since that was still ringing in her ears. She took a deep breath and went at it, hit a wrong note and kept going. Her old Yamaha sounded tinny, no resonance, after Freddie's Martin. She stopped in mid-phrase and didn't dare to look at him.

For a moment no one said anything. Then Freddie said, "You need work."

"Oh, I *know* it. Like from Day One."

He smiled his rare smile. "More like Day Three. You want to come to my place around six thirty next Wednesday?"

"Yes." It was all she could trust herself to say.

"Tell her how much," Abner said. "Be practical."

Freddie was putting his guitar in its case, handling it with the kind of tender care a mother gives her infant. "Don't know yet. It all depends."

She didn't dare ask what it depended on. She didn't care what it cost. She'd pay all she could get her hands on. "Where do you live?"

"I'll take you," Abner said. "Eric or me or both of us."

Marcie stood up cautiously. Her stomach was still a bit queasy, but the room stayed on its proper plane. Abner came over and unexpectedly put his hands on her shoulders. His face, so close, looked older than she had thought. There were tiny lines around his eyes and mouth and a faint scar along the left side of his jaw.

"When you get up tomorrow," he said, "you're going to be thirsty. Don't drink any water or you'll get smashed all over again."

"I already told her that," Eric said.

Freddie squeezed Eric's shoulder with his big hand. "The man of experience." He strode to the door, looking too big for the room. "So long, y'all."

On the way home Marcie said, "I feel as if I just hit a watershed in my life."

"That was a champagne shed."

"No, I'm serious. I think you just changed my life. I'm going to learn to play the guitar right. I'm going to stay in Austin."

Eric yawned. "Glad to hear it. Let me off at the next corner, by the street light."

"I can drive you home."

"No, it's just a couple blocks from here. You know your way all right? First right, and the house is second from the end of the cul de sac."

"I can find it. Eric, thanks an awful lot."

"For the watershed? You're welcome. I always pass them out to my friends." He swung out of the car. "See ya. Hey, where will you be?"

"At Kate's till she gets home."

"Right." He waved and disappeared in the dark.

# 16

There was a light showing at the bottom of her mother's door. Marcie was tempted to ignore it, but her mother always said she couldn't go to sleep till Marcie got in. Whether it was true or not, it was simpler to report in. Besides . . . Marcie suddenly forgot the music that was flooding her mind and faced reality; she had to tell her mother that she was staying in Austin. Mom's flight left in the morning.

She knocked and waited for her mother's voice. With any luck she'd be asleep. But she wasn't. She was in bed reading a detective story. She always looked smaller and pale without her makeup, more vulnerable somehow.

"I couldn't go to sleep till you came in," she said. "Where did you go?" She said it conversationally, not accusingly.

"John's cousin Eric took me to hear some musicians." Unable to conceal her enthusiasm, she added, "Oh, Mom, they were wonderful. One of them is going to give me lessons."

Her mother raised her eyebrows. "Nana mentioned that you might stay on a week or so. Of course you hadn't told me, so I had no way of knowing."

"I wasn't sure." She sat down on her mother's bed. "I'm going to stay in Austin awhile. Longer than a week. I really want those lessons."

"Honey, country music is not a terribly lofty ambition."

"It's not country. It's bluegrass. It's quite different. It's . . ." But her mother wasn't listening.

"I've decided not to rush off myself," she said. "I cancelled my flight."

That was the last thing Marcie had expected. "But why? What would you do here?"

"What will Nana do? What will you do? What does anyone do? I want to see the LBJ Library and the Johnson ranch; and Mrs. Angell, one of the Fenton relatives, says I should visit Fredericksburg. There are lots of things to do. I think I deserve a vacation. Your father goes off to the Orient and heaven knows where, and I sit at home. So anyway . . ." She took off her reading glasses and patted the blanket with a little complacent gesture. "So I'll just get a double room at the Driskill, and you and I can do some shopping and sightseeing. I might just drive home with you instead of flying. That flight was so crowded, and Dallas–Forth Worth airport is so confusing."

"Mother." Marcie took a deep breath. "I'm not going to stay at the Driskill. I'm going to use Kate's apartment till she gets home, and then I'll get one of my own. And I really don't want to sightsee."

"Well, we'll talk about it in the morning." Her mother snuggled down comfortably. "You were a little tipsy at the reception, Marcie. I do hope you'll be careful about drinking. You've probably inherited your father's unfortunate tendency that way. He never could hold his liquor."

Marcie felt like screaming. This whole thing was turning out all wrong. It had never occurred to her that her mother would not go home in the morning. She said goodnight and went to her own room. How did she handle this? She took Kate's key out of her purse, and the check her father had given her. She was surprised at how large it was. He really meant it when he said he wanted her to stay away from home. It would help—the money. She'd be able to get a room somewhere and keep herself in groceries. But her mother . . . how long would she stay? Marcie felt outmaneuvered.

She got into her pajamas and robe and opened the door that led to the pool. The moon was making a silver streak across the water. She went out and started to sit down, but realized suddenly that she was not alone. Aunt Meg was huddled in a deck chair.

"Oh, I'm sorry," Marcie said. "I didn't know there was anyone here."

"That's all right, dear. Sit down. I was just looking at the moon."

Marcie sat down next to her. "It was a great wedding and reception and everything. I bet you're tired."

Aunt Meg took a moment to answer. "It's been a long day. But it *was* nice, wasn't it. I think they're going to be happy. Peg is a sweet girl." She lit a cigarette, and the end glowed like a tiny falling star as she moved her arm. "It was the beginning of something, and the end of something."

Marcie wasn't sure what she meant, so she waited.

"Joe and I parted company today."

Marcie was startled. In spite of what Eric had said, she had had no idea that he meant this. "I'm so sorry," she said. "I didn't realize . . ."

"No. Few people did. Joe loves to have things civilized, as he puts it. We've been agreed on the separation for some time, but it seemed better to wait until after the wedding. Though his choice of this day to depart seemed to me a touch melodramatic. He's going to marry one of his graduate students. It's curious, isn't it, how often men look for a younger woman as they themselves begin to age. It seems as if they are more frightened of age than we are." Her voice was calm, almost remote.

Marcie thought of her own mother's hysterics. Different people certainly reacted differently to similar situations. "I hope you're not unhappy," she said. "But I guess that's a stupid thing to say."

"No, sweetie, not stupid. I am more sad than unhappy. Sadness isn't quite as traumatic, I suppose. Maybe one learns not to expect happiness as a given. When it comes, it's best, perhaps, to hold it tight and store it away so you can remember it afterward. I have a lot of very nice memories." She sat up straighter and made a decisive gesture. "And I intend to be happy again from time to time. Nothing is the end of the world, except perhaps the actual end of the world."

On an impulse, Marcie said, "Would you mind if I talked to you about something? About me, actually. Maybe you don't feel like hearing somebody else's problems . . ."

"It's just what I need to hear."

Marcie told her about her decision to stay in Austin and about her mother's unexpected plans.

Aunt Meg was silent for a few minutes. "I never had a daughter. I'm sure it must be quite different from having a son. I always expected John to be gone; in fact, I thought it would happen sooner than it did. I don't mind that. Of course he will be in town, at least for a while, so it's easy for me to say I don't mind. I suspect your mother felt betrayed when your father left; it's easy to feel that way. And now your wanting to go must seem, unconsciously, like a second betrayal." She put out her cigarette in the ashtray beside her. "But you have to do it, Marcie. It will be hard on you because you're a loving person, but love doesn't necessarily require us to give in to the ones we love." She gathered her robe around her and stood up, looking tall in the darkness. "Whatever I can do to help, I will. If she would like to stay here, she is welcome. And you are too, any time. But I suppose, basically, you have to do this alone." She leaned down and kissed Marcie's cheek. "Whenever you feel like talking, come see me. And thank you for talking to me tonight. I was feeling very sorry for myself when you came out here. I've stopped that nonsense, at least for now."

Marcie sat by the pool awhile longer. Why did life have to get so complicated? Everybody's wishes and needs colliding with everybody else's. It was exhausting. She yawned and went in to bed, feeling that nothing was resolved.

# 17

It was Abner who picked up Marcie to take her to her first lesson. He was looking jaunty in tight white jeans, a blue T-shirt, and a yachting cap on the back of his close-cropped reddish hair. Marcie thought he looked like a man about town from the Twenties, a Scott Fitzgerald character, maybe.

"Tell you what," he said, flopping down in one of Kate's comfortable chairs, "you drive your car, and I'll lead the way, like a police escort for a VIP, you know? Then I'll be off. I have a date with a sailboat at the lake. And you can find your way home by yourself, okay?"

"Sure. I could probably find my way there by myself, too. I hope I'm not lousing up your time schedule." She wondered if the date with the boat included a girl.

"Nope. Not a bit. It's hard to find Freddie's place. Hernando's Hideaway kind of place. So, shall we take off?"

She had to drive faster than she liked to keep up with Abner. He wove in and out of traffic in long graceful swoops, like some kind of motorized bird.

But she was glad he had made himself her guide. Freddie's tiny house was tucked away on a street that she would have had trouble finding. It was a very neat-looking little house, with a small mowed lawn in front and a long narrow yard in the back. No other house was very close, which must be an advantage, she thought, if you are a musician. Neighbors could be a problem. Even at home Mrs. McGraw sometimes made pointed remarks about Marcie's tapes and even, on summer days with open windows, her guitar music.

She thanked Abner, who unexpectedly leaned sideways in the saddle of his BMW and kissed her. Then he roared off. She stood for a moment looking after him. He probably kissed girls all over the place. But it had been nice.

Freddie's living room was small and filled almost to bursting with a couch, a torn leather chair, a straight kitchen chair, and all kinds of musical equipment: stereo, speakers, mikes, amps, several guitars, a dobro, an electric bass guitar, and a mandolin. It looked like a recording studio.

The walls were painted pale green, and there were straw rugs on the floor. In spite of the clutter, the place was clean.

She stood in the middle of the room clutching her guitar, not knowing just what to do.

"Sit down," Freddie said in his deep voice. "Want a beer?"

"No, thanks." She watched him take one out of the tiny refrigerator in the adjoining kitchen. He brought the bottle into the room and sprawled on the sofa.

"Play me something," he said.

She took her guitar out of the case, her hands trembling. She was trying to think of everything that Ossipee Joe had ever taught her. "It's just a cheap guitar," she said. "I never realized the difference till I went to a festival in New Orleans, and then when I heard yours. That Martin is so deep and rich, it makes mine sound like a cigarbox with rubber bands."

He waited patiently, without comment.

"I guess I'll play 'John Hardy.'" She wished her voice didn't sound so high and girlish. It didn't usually sound like that, did it? Like some nervous little kid. "Because I know 'John Hardy' the best."

"Fire when ready," he said. He leaned his head back and closed his eyes.

She clenched her teeth and hit a strong opening chord. As soon as she got into it, she forgot about being nervous. When you played bluegrass, it took all your concentration. Once or twice she hit a wrong note, but she kept going.

When she had finished, her nervousness flooded back. He didn't say anything for a long minute, and she was sure he was trying to think how tactfully to get rid of her.

Then he said, "You're thumb-picking. Ever use a flat pick?"

"A little. This man I knew gave me one, but I never learned to do a lot with it."

He got up and found a flat pick, the flat oval kind that the player holds between his fingers instead of the one, like hers, that fits over the thumb. He gave it to her and then picked up one of his own guitars, a Gibson. "I'm going to play 'Red-Haired Boy.' You listen, and then we'll try it together."

His calmness had a calming effect on her. She listened intently as he played. Then he nodded to her, and she began to play with him. She went at it too hard and broke a string. He stopped and got her the Martin. "Try this one."

She couldn't believe the difference. It was so much easier to play, so much louder and more resonant.

While they rested later, Freddie got a set of strings and showed her how to change them efficiently. She had always been awkward at it. He wrote down the name of the kind of strings she should have. "They're about seven bucks a set."

"I love your guitar. What a difference!"

"You can play it while you're here, if you want to. Okay, let's run through 'Love, Please Come Home.'" He played it once for her, and then they played together. "Don't stop if you make a mistake. Keep going."

Marcie couldn't believe it later when she glanced at the old alarm clock on the table and saw that they had been playing for two hours. She was tired, and her fingers were beginning to blister, but she couldn't remember ever having been so happy.

"Good enough." He smiled at her, his eyes smiling more than his mouth did. He was so big, she thought he might have played football.

She asked him, and he laughed. "I guess every guy as big as I am gets asked that. As a matter of fact, I was on the swim team."

"Where?"

"Baylor. I was thinking about being a preacher, but I dropped out. Now I fix other people's foreign cars to keep up with alimony payments." He stood up, and the room seemed to shrink. "You're pretty good, Marcie. You need to practice a whole lot. If you improve, maybe you and Abner and I could play some gigs together."

Marcie stopped in the act of putting her guitar in the case. "Are you serious?"

"Why not? If you want to."

"If I want to!"

"But you need to work. And I mean hard work. Why don't you come here every other night for a while. Can you do that?"

"Of course I can. I'd love to. Listen, you haven't told me how much to pay you."

"Oh, let's worry about that later. I got a name in my head for a group. I want to call us Texas Instruments."

She laughed. "That's great. Shall I come at the same time?"

"Right. Can you find your way home?"

She was in such a state of euphoria, she didn't care whether she found her way home or not, but after a few wrong turns and dead-end streets, she got back to Kate's apartment.

The phone was ringing when she got in. It was her mother.

"Where in the world have you been? I've been worried sick."

Marcie was too happy to be irritated. "I was taking a guitar lesson. I told you."

"You've been gone for hours. Who is this person?"

"He's a friend of Eric's. And Mom, he is wonderful. I learned so much, just in one night. I'm going to practice like crazy and take a lesson every other night."

"He's bilking you." It was one of her mother's favorite words. She had never heard anyone else use it.

"No, he isn't. We may form a group after I get good enough." She enjoyed hearing herself say "after" she was good enough, not "if."

"What kind of a group? I hope you don't mean you'd play in bars and things. Your grandmother took me to a place called Jalapeño Joe's, can you believe it? It was just a dive, a beer garden, with a group of people playing crazy, so-called music. Your grandmother loved it. Sometimes I really wonder if there isn't a touch of senility—"

Marcie cut her off. "Mom, I'm really tired. I'll talk to you tomorrow, okay? Have a good night's sleep." She hung up before her mother could protest.

The phone rang again when she was in the shower, but she didn't answer it.

## 18

"I tried to call you," Abner said.

"I didn't answer because I thought it was my mother."

"When is your mother going home?" Abner put down one of Marcie's grocery bags in the tiny kitchen of the apartment she had found three blocks away from Kate's. Kate was coming home from the hospital in the afternoon.

"I wish I knew," Marcie said. Then, feeling disloyal, she added, "Pretty soon, I guess. My grandmother and her friend have gone down to Galveston for a few days, and Mom is feeling neglected."

"Does she know you're going to stay all year?" He flopped onto the sofa that made into a bed and looked around the room. "This isn't too bad for a furnished pad. Not that it has any character, sort of like a motel room." He had showed up the day after her first lesson and had volunteered to help her move. Not, as she told him, that there was much to move. Herself, her big canvas bag, her guitar. But he had come anyway, and they had gone grocery shopping.

"Mom doesn't really like Austin," she said, not answering his question because she didn't want to explain that with her mother she did things one small step at a time. "She hates the heat. But my grandmother loves it. She took Mom to Jalapeño Joe's to hear Butch Hancock. Mom hated it, but Nana had the time of her life. She bought a record that he autographed to me."

"He's real good. We'll go hear him some night. He plays around at different places. Used to be a terrific place called emmajoe's that had fantastic music, from Rosalie Sorrels to Ponty Bone and the Squeezetones. But it folded, alas."

She was making coffee. "I've been practicing so hard I've got blisters."

"That's all right. They'll turn into calluses and be permanent." He came and leaned on the counter, watching her with his teasing grin. "No respectable guy will marry a woman with calluses on her fingers."

"So I'll stay single."

"Atta girl. Avoid all entangling alliances. George Washington said that."

She glanced at him. "Are you putting me on?"

"No, I swear, he did. I learned that in the eighth grade in Germantown, Phila-del-phy-ay, P A."

"Is that where you're from?" She knew nothing at all about him. He always changed the subject when she asked about his life.

"Long years ago."

99

Eric had told her that Abner's name wasn't really Abner Frothingham. "He picked that out of a Boston society column."

"Why did he do that?" she had asked.

Eric shrugged. "Dunno. Abner's ways are mysterious ways. Some guy that knows him said he used to be in the Navy and he went AWOL, but I don't know if that's true. And don't ever mention it."

Abner intrigued her. Sometimes she amused herself comparing him to Vin, or to Tony, the guy she had gone out with a lot last year. Abner wasn't like anyone else. He was like a leprechaun or something not quite human.

Later, when she was washing out the coffee cups, Abner came up behind her and put his arms around her waist and kissed the back of her neck. He was always so unserious, so teasing about everything, she didn't know quite how to handle him. She liked having him kiss her, but something in the back of her mind told her not to get involved.

She made a joke herself and handed him a dish towel. "Get to work. This is the age of equal rights."

She had decided to cook a dinner that she could take over for Manuel and Kate, on Kate's first night back in her apartment. She put Abner to work helping her prepare a potato and chive casserole and a roast chicken. He tucked a dish towel into the waistband of his shorts and chopped vegetables and peeled mushrooms for stuffing, then peeled potatoes for the casserole.

They read recipes in the *Austin Statesman*, looking for a dessert, but in the end Abner went out and bought a lot of fruit. Most desserts had sugar, and that wouldn't do for Kate.

Manuel had agreed to call them when he brought Kate home. Soon after his call, she and Abner covered the dishes with layers of aluminum foil and drove over to Kate's.

Kate was lying on the sofa when they got there. She looked pale and a little thin in the face, but otherwise surprisingly well. She seemed very glad to see them and was touched by their thoughtfulness in bringing the meal.

"Stay and eat it with us," she said.

But Marcie thought Kate and Manuel should have their evening together without company. "Abner has promised to take me to the best Mexican restaurant in town." She kissed Kate on the forehead. "Thank you for the apartment. It was a lifesaver."

"I'm glad. I had a card from Peg and John. They sound as if they're having a ball. Come see me tomorrow if you have time."

Marcie was quiet through the meal at the little Mexican restaurant on the east side of town.

"What's on your mind?" Abner said.

"Kate. She probably won't live terribly long."

"Probably or might not?"

"Well, I guess might not."

"Who knows how long any of us will live?"

He stared into the dimness of the restaurant for so long that she finally asked, "What do you mean? Like having a car crash or something?"

"I was in the service once. Remember the ships that bombed the hills of Lebanon?"

"Do you mean you were on one of those?"

He didn't answer directly. "People are getting killed all over the place, innocent people, as if they were rabbits or mosquitoes."

She wanted to ask questions, but he hardly spoke again during the meal. Earlier he had mentioned taking her to hear

Uncle Walt's band, downtown, but he didn't mention it again. When she dropped him off at his apartment house, he seemed so depressed, it worried her. She tried to think of something cheerful to say, but he said goodnight, brushed off her thanks, and ran into the house.

When she got home, she called Freddie and told him how depressed Abner seemed.

"He gets that way," Freddie said. "Sometimes he's in a black mood for days. Then he comes out of it as if nothing had happened, and he's all jokes again. Don't worry about it. There's nothing anyone can do. Listen, I was going to call you; we've got a chance to play a gig a week from Saturday night. It's just a dim little joint up on Lamar, but a gig is a gig. How do you feel about it?"

"How do I feel! I'd love it!"

"I'll try to get tomorrow afternoon off so we can practice. I hope Abner will come, too, but if he's off on a dejection jag, you and I can practice. I'll call you around noon."

Marcie hung up and got her guitar. She was practicing so hard that at first she didn't hear the phone. It was her mother.

"Darling, I've got tickets for us for a week from Saturday night for a performance of *Coriolanus*. I played Volumnia, you know, in our graduation play. My, how it takes me back! 'There's no man in the world More bound to's mother; yet here he lets me prate Like one i' the stocks. Thou hast never in the life Show'd thy dear mother any courtesy . . .' Oh, it was a great part."

"Mom," Marcie said, "I have a gig Saturday night . . ."

"A what? Oh, and I asked John's mother to go to lunch with us tomorrow at that Old Pecan place on Sixth Street. It looks respectable. And she's going to take us to the LBJ

Library afterward. I never had any use for LBJ, but I'd like to see the library. History is history, after all. So why don't you pick me up at twelve thirty—"

"Mother! Please listen. First, I am sorry but I can't go to *Coriolanus* because we have a playing date. It's our first real gig and it's very important."

There was a silence. Then her mother said, "I don't know what a gig is."

"It's a date to play. And I can't go to lunch and all that. I'd love to, but I've got to practice like crazy. In fact, I'll probably be practicing with Abner and Freddie all afternoon tomorrow, if Freddie can get a half day off. It's terribly important."

"And dates with me are not important, of course."

"Mother, I don't have a date with you. This is the first I've heard of either of these things. You go with Aunt Meg. You don't need me. Maybe she'd like to go to *Coriolanus*."

"I am not trying to make a bosom friend of John's mother," she said coldly. "I am simply repaying a social obligation. If you refuse to go with me, then of course I shan't go."

"But why not? You want to see it. Ask Nana."

"She is off somewhere with her friend. She wouldn't go anyway."

Marcie felt trapped. For a moment she thought of compromising on the lunch. But it would be an entire afternoon of practice lost, and she couldn't afford it. It was awfully soon for her to be playing in public anyway, even if it was some out-of-the-way little bar. If she gave in, her mother might stay here for months, counting on Marcie to entertain her. "I'm sorry, Mother. I can't do it."

Her mother hung up without answering. She was probably

in tears. She would get a migraine headache. She would get that mysterious pain in her ear. Marcie reached for the phone, then stopped. If she gave an inch, she'd end up giving all the way. It had been happening that way for years.

She unplugged the phone and went back to her guitar. But it was a while before she could concentrate. She couldn't remember ever before having flat-out refused even to compromise when her mother wanted her to change her plans. She wasn't sure whether what she felt most strongly was guilt or triumph.

# 19

Her mother presumably went to lunch and the LBJ with Aunt Meg, but she did not mention it, and Marcie decided she was not going to bring up painful subjects unnecessarily.

On Sunday she took her mother to church, and they had breakfast afterward at the Marriott. Nana was still off somewhere with her friend Bridget.

"You'd think she would at least send a card," Marcie's mother said. "She could drop dead, and we'd never know it."

"I guess someone would tell us," Marcie said. "Anyway I can't see Nana dropping dead."

"None of us are immortal, you know."

Marcie concentrated on the little packages of raw brown

sugar in the sugar bowl. She loved that kind of sugar. "I wonder if they carry this at Wheatsville." Kate had introduced her to the interesting coop food store on Guadaloupe, near the university.

"I hate health food stores," her mother said. "They charge outrageous prices and call everything organic."

Marcie tried again, looking for a neutral subject. "That's a nice little church, isn't it."

"Too small," her mother said. "I like a big churchy church."

Marcie sighed. "Well, we can try St. David's next week." Next week. She wanted to ask how much longer her mother was going to stay. It seemed to be going on and on.

"I've been having that ear pain," her mother said

"You ought to go see Dr. Marshall." Maybe this was a way to get her to go home. "He helped you before, didn't he?"

"Helped, no. He just fed me pain-killers that upset my stomach. He has no idea what the cause is. I may go to a doctor Mrs. Henley mentioned."

She had met Mrs. Henley at the reception, and Mrs. Henley had invited her to fill in at a bridge club party.

"He's a chiropractor." She waited for Marcie's reaction. When none came, she said, "Your father says chiropractors are fakes."

Marcie shrugged. She wasn't going to get dragged into that old battle. "Go to whomever helps you."

Her mother summoned the waitress for more coffee. "Where did you say you are playing your guitar Saturday night?"

Marcie felt a tremor of alarm. "I didn't say. I don't really know. It's out at the other end of town."

"How can you play there if you don't know where it is?"

"That's Freddie's problem. He arranges the dates. I just tag along."

106

"I hope it's a respectable place."

"Well, it's not the Driskill, I'm sure. Or the Ritz." Sometimes her mother's snobbery was more than she could take in silence. She looked at her watch. She had a date to go swimming with Kate, and then she had to practice at Freddie's. "Shall we go?"

"I just started this cup of coffee. Are you in such a rush you can't even relax for breakfast?"

Marcie was late for her swimming date. She apologized to Kate as they drove out to the health club where Kate swam. "My mother wouldn't quit eating breakfast."

"That's all right." Kate was looking a lot better. She swam every day, and she had taken Marcie with her once before. She spent an exact hour in the pool, timing herself with a lap-swimmer's watch, so many laps at a slow pace to warm up, so many laps at increased speed, checking her pulse, and then a slowing down period, and finally fifteen minutes in the sauna. Marcie was impressed by her discipline.

When they were in the sauna, Kate said, "Would it be okay if Manuel and I came to hear your gig?"

"Sure, I'd love it. But I think it's kind of a dive."

"That's all right. We've been in dives before. I think Manuel wants to talk you and Freddie and Abner and maybe Eric into playing for a legal defense fund benefit in September. Do you think the guys would go for it?"

"I know or at least I think I know Freddie would. And Eric. I'm never sure of anything about Abner. We could play without him if we had to, I guess."

"Good. Manuel has big plans. He wants to get two or three groups, so you can spell each other, and have music all evening. It'll probably be outdoors, maybe in one of the parks."

"I'd love to do something like that, something useful."

"I saw Freddie on campus the other day. He said you're getting very good."

Marcie was pleased. Freddie had never said that to her, but he had nodded a few times as if he approved. He worked her very hard, and she practiced for hours.

When Kate dropped her off, she said, "Maybe Peg and John will be home by Saturday night."

"That would be nice," Marcie said, although she really hoped they wouldn't. She had enough to be nervous about without the possibility of her sister's being in the bar. "Peg's card to me didn't say much, but I guess you don't write home when you're on your honeymoon."

She had just enough time to eat a sandwich and change her clothes before it was time to go to Freddie's. Abner had not been to the practice sessions, and when Freddie had called his apartment there had been no answer.

"We better be prepared for having just the two of us, at that gig," Freddie said. "I'd like to take Eric, but there'd be trouble about his age. Anyway, his mother might not let him. It's kind of a tough workingman's bar. Nothing wrong with it, just not what you'd call elegant."

Marcie put out a small fervent prayer that her mother wouldn't find out where it was and decide to come.

She and Freddie got to work on the numbers Freddie had decided they would do. In some of them she and Freddie sang in harmony.

At about nine o'clock, when they were taking a break, Abner arrived, bursting in without knocking, keyed up to a high pitch of energy. He was on such a high, Marcie wondered if he'd been fooling around with drugs, although he had told her several times that he didn't do drugs. "My highs are high enough and my lows are low enough without drugs," he had said.

He insisted that they end their break at once and plunge into practice. Freddie tried to slow Abner down, but that was impossible. And he played with astonishing brilliance and verve.

They finished "Billy in the Low Ground" with a long banjo break that was so breathtaking Marcie and Freddie looked at each other and said in unison, "Wowie!" Abner laughed.

"Man, you keep getting better and better," Freddie said.

Abner made a sweeping bow. "Thank you, sir. Come on, what are we waiting for?" He struck a loud chord and went into "I Don't Believe You've Met My Baby." This was one of Marcie's favorites.

Abner went right on, hardly stopping for a second. "Gold Rush," "Blue Ridge Mountain Home," "Can't You Hear Me Callin' You," "Sweet Georgia Brown."

"Whoa!" Marcie fell back into the nearest chair. "Wait up. I can't take it. Gimme air."

Abner grabbed an old Stetson of Freddie's and fanned her energetically. Freddie went into the kitchen and opened some beer.

"I'm taking this lady out for a breath of air," Abner announced. "Be back in four and a half minutes." He dragged Marcie to her feet and took her out into the grassy area behind Freddie's house. It was pitch dark, except for a thin slit of light from Freddie's kitchen window. Abner pulled Marcie up to him and held her painfully tight, her face pressed against his.

She was startled and tried to make a joke of it. "Hey, I thought you brought me out here for air. I'm not breathing."

He kissed her hard on the mouth, and when he let up for a

moment, she tried to pull back. Abner was attractive and exciting, but this was a bit much. His teeth had cut her lip. She could taste the tiny trickle of blood.

"Let up, Abner. Come on, quit."

But he wasn't quitting. He pushed her against an old picnic table and forced her onto her back. "I missed you, babe."

She tried to fight him off, but he had her pinned down. Angry and frightened, she wanted to yell, but she couldn't get her face free of his, and there was no breath left in her lungs. Abner was yanking her T-shirt up with his left hand and holding her wrists over her head with his other hand. Surely Freddie would come out if they didn't go in in a minute, but how long did it take to get raped?

The night was stiflingly hot, and there was a strong smell of flowers, she wasn't sure what kind. Why was she thinking about what kind of flowers she was smelling? She put all the strength she had left into pulling her hands free, got Abner off balance, and brought her knee up hard.

He yelled and fell off her, bending over and clutching himself. Suddenly Freddie loomed up in the dark, looking twice as big as usual.

"What's going on here?" He looked at Marcie, who was struggling to get off the table and pull her clothes together. Then he grabbed Abner by the front of his shirt and shook him. Abner screamed. Freddie threw him backward into the bushes. "You ever bother Marcie again, and I'll tear you apart," he said. "I'm not kidding." He turned to Marcie and said, "Come on." He stalked ahead of her, a long-legged, broad giant in the darkness.

Neither of them spoke. She went into the tiny bathroom and washed her face and hands, then sat down on the edge of the bathtub. She was shaking so hard, her teeth chattered. It wasn't as if she had never had to fight a guy off before. Any girl who went out was likely to run into that situation. But she had never come that close to losing the fight. Usually you could make the guy believe you meant no after a few minutes. But Abner had acted like a crazy man, as if he wasn't even aware of who she was. As if he didn't even know her.

Finally she got up, combed her hair, and went out into the other room. There was no sign of Abner. Even his banjo was gone. She didn't ask where he was. Freddie had fixed her a gin and tonic, and she drank it gratefully, although she normally hated gin. She used to say it tasted like battery acid, although who knew what battery acid tasted like.

Freddie was frowning. "I thought he'd got over that kind of stuff," he said.

"You mean he does that often?"

"Not any more. I didn't think he did. He used to have these spells when he'd go kind of crazy. A long dark period and then higher'n a kite, like he was tonight, and then something like this. I should have realized when he came in tonight like a two-hundred-watt lightbulb. When he was in the Navy, they put him in sick bay, and he had a Navy psychologist working on him, but he broke out and went AWOL somehow, God knows how."

"Will he be all right now? I mean, he won't get in trouble?"

"I don't think so. By the time he left just now, he was like sobered up. It's as if he's on a drug, and all of a sudden it wears off and he's horrified at what's he done. He'll go home and grieve."

She drank the gin slowly, letting the warmth relax her. "It was scary."

"I blame myself. I should have kept an eye on him. But it's been a long time since he busted loose like that." He shook his head. "But man, can't he play when he's wired up!"

"Yes. It was amazing."

"How are you going to feel about playing with him in the group? We could dump him—"

"No. I'll be all right. I just won't be alone with him."

"I'll see to that. But are you sure? He was worrying about that when he left. Kept saying he blew it. He really likes you."

"I liked him, too."

He stood up. "Well, we better call it a night. You want me to take you home?"

"No, of course not."

"You don't need to worry about him bothering you again. I'm sure of that. But you might feel better if I trailed you home."

"No, really. I'm okay. He ought to see a doctor though, oughtn't he?"

"He's scared he might talk too much and the Navy'd find him. I doubt they're still looking for him, but he thinks they are. Has nightmares about it." He walked her out to her car. "Lock your car doors. Not on account of Abner, just on account of good sense."

"I will. Thanks for coming to the rescue."

He smiled. "You were doing all right by yourself." He put her guitar in the back seat. "I guess it must be hell being a woman sometimes." He gave her shoulder a fatherly pat. "Get a good night's sleep."

She drove home trying not to imagine that every car behind her was following her. When she had parked the car, she walked fast to the apartment house door, fumbled with the

lock, and dropped the key. By the time she got the door unlocked and was safely inside, she was shaking again.

She looked at herself in the bathroom mirror: pale and her
hair was a mess. Pull yourself together, for heaven's sake,
she said. And stop thinking it was somehow your fault.

But it took her a long time and two cups of hot milk to get
to sleep.

# 20

She had been dreaming that the doorbell was ringing when she woke up and realized that it was in fact ringing, a long, steady ring, someone holding a finger on the button. She was up, in her bathrobe, and on her way to the door before she was awake enough to realize that it was not smart to open the door to someone unknown at three o'clock in the morning.

She stood in front of the door, hoping the ringing would go away, hoping it wasn't audible to her neighbors. They were understanding about her guitar practice, especially since they worked all day and she usually practiced during the day, but a shrill bell waking them at this hour would strain anyone's neighborly feelings.

She knocked lightly on the door. "What do you want?" she said. Her next line was going to be, "I'm calling the cops."

The ringing stopped at once. "It's me . . ." The voice said a name that sounded like "Jack" or something. Then he said, "It's Abner. Can I come in?"

She leaned against the door, feeling suddenly weak. "Please, Abner. It's three o'clock. You'll wake up the whole building."

"I'm sorry. I didn't know what time it was. I've been riding around." He sounded different, subdued, almost humble. "Could I talk to you a few minutes? I won't . . . I'll go away if you want me to, but I'd like to talk to you."

The feelings of fondness she had felt for him fought against the revulsion and fear he had caused. After a minute she opened the door. "We can't stand here talking through the door," she said. "But it's really late, Abner."

"I know. I won't stay long." He even looked different. Older, tired, depressed. But it wasn't the remote dark mood she had seen in him before. He looked pleading.

"Do you want some coffee?" She led the way into the kitchen, unconsciously wrapping her bathrobe closer around her and tightening the cord. She put some water on the stove to boil and got the instant coffee and two cups. "I have milk, no cream."

"Black." He sat in one of the chairs, huddling as if he were cold, but the night was warm and humid. "I'm sorry I woke you up. I had to talk to you. I forgot about the time."

"That's all right." She felt tense. It was hard to talk to him. Even hard to look at him. For some crazy reason she felt as if she ought to apologize to him for the unpleasant scene in Freddie's yard.

There was a long, uncomfortable silence. She poured hot

water into the two cups and stirred the coffee crystals, put some milk into her own. She thought of her mother saying, "If you drink coffee after five o'clock, you'll be awake all night." It was like her mother to think that if coffee kept her awake, it would keep everyone awake.

He wrapped both his thin hands around the coffee cup and stared into it. His fingers broadened at the tips, with calluses like her own. She thought about how brilliantly he had played earlier that night. It was odd to realize that it was all the same night; it seemed like ages ago.

"Are you okay, Abner?" Her other emotions were wiped out in a wave of pity for him. He looked so broken down, all his cheerful arrogance gone.

"My name isn't really Abner," he said. "It's Matt. Matthew Thomas Blake. Doesn't that sound like a nineteenth century English novel?"

"Do you want me to call you Matt?"

"Not in front of the Shore Police." He managed a weak smile. "No, it doesn't matter what you call me. I'm just glad you're still calling me anything. I can't tell you how sorry, how ashamed—" His voice broke.

"Come on," she said gently, "forget it." It was embarrassing to see him like this. She wished he would say what he had to say and leave.

"All right. But I wanted you to know. I turn into somebody else sometimes. I haven't had that happen for a couple of years. Two years, a month, and three days, to be exact. I kind of black out, and afterward I'm not sure what I've done. This time Freddie made it abundantly clear. I thought he was going to break my bones. Should have, I guess."

"Don't," she said. "You're feeling sorry for yourself."

"I ought to go to a shrink, but there are certain obstacles. Money, for one."

"There are health clinics," she said. "Why don't you ask Kate's friend, Manuel? He knows about things like that."

He nodded, but she didn't think he was really listening. "Mainly, I just wanted to tell you that you don't need to be scared of me. When something like that hits me, it doesn't usually recur for a long time. I kind of build up to it, with depression and all that. I should have seen it coming, but I never do, somehow." He drank all the contents of his cup in one long drink. "I'll be okay now." He got up. "Thanks for letting me in and for listening. I think a lot of you, Marcie. You're the last person I'd have—" He broke off and shook his head. "Sorry I woke you up."

She followed him to the door. "Are you going home now? Get some sleep?"

"Yeah. I'll probably sleep all day. Tell Freddie I'll show up tomorrow night to practice. No problems." He gave her a quick, sad little smile and left.

She locked the door and leaned against it. Poor Abner. Poor Matthew Thomas Blake. Manic-depressive? She tried to remember what little she had learned in Psych. Not enough to put anybody in a category, that was for sure.

She went to bed and lay awake until the first flat gray light of another hot day showed up outside her window. People got screwed up and who knew why? She should remember that, when her mother irritated and exasperated her. Who could tell what genes, what long-forgotten experiences, what obscure hankypanky going on in the brain, made her cling so to other people? Marcie made a resolution to be more patient.

117

# 21

It seemed to Marcie that everything happened on the day of their first gig. Nana and her friend Bridget returned from wherever they had been this time, and Peg and John phoned from Dallas–Fort Worth to say they would be home that afternoon. And Marcie had to take her mother to an appointment with an acupuncturist. Someone she had met somewhere had talked her out of the chiropractor and turned her on to acupuncture.

Marcie, who had hoped for a quiet do-nothing day in which to pull herself together, felt frazzled. Her mother was annoyed because Marcie wouldn't tell her the name of the bar. In fact Marcie had made a point of not paying any attention to the name or the location, so she could truthfully say she didn't know, but her mother didn't believe her anyway.

Late in the afternoon, when everything urgent seemed to have been taken care of, she broke a string on her guitar and had to restring it. Then she began to worry about what to wear. She had changed her mind a dozen times. Freddie had said, "Jeans. T-shirt. Nothing attention-getting." And Abner had said, "Neat but not gaudy, as the old lady said when she kissed the cow."

Abner seemed to be all right again, and the constraint that had been in the air the first time they all practiced had disappeared, although Marcie noticed that Freddie was careful not to leave them alone together. She knew Abner noticed it too, and that it hurt.

She unplugged the phone, tried to take a short nap, failed, and began to dress. She decided finally on her white jeans, a cobalt blue cotton shirt, her new leather sandals. Neat but not gaudy. She had to think about comfort, about being able to move easily in her clothes when she played, and the shirt was one of her favorites for that.

She tried to eat something, but she was too nervous. She drank a glass of milk and ate half a peanut butter sandwich for protein, then stuck a granola bar in her shoulder pack.

Freddie picked her up in his old VW van, with the instruments and equipment. He was going to play his mandolin for a few of the numbers.

"I brought the Gibson for you," he said.

"Oh, good!" Playing Freddie's Gibson and Martin at his house had spoiled her for her old Yamaha. "Thanks, Freddie." Her father had written her that he would send her a check every month, and when she got the next one, she would get Freddie to help her find a good guitar. She wanted to tell him that, but right now she was too tense to talk much.

Abner's motorcycle was already there when they got to

the bar. It was called Po' Boy's, and it was on a side street, small and dingy. "Just a little old bar," as Freddie had said. Marcie was glad her mother didn't know where it was.

Abner was sitting at the bar talking to the bartender when they came in. The television was on, and several men in working clothes were grouped at the end, watching a rerun of "Remington Steele." A middle-aged woman sat alone at the other end, drinking a beer.

Harry, the bartender, was a small worried-looking man. "Business'll pick up," he said to Marcie, without much conviction. "By the time you're ready, she'll pick up." He offered her a beer, but she shook her head.

"You know how we get paid," Abner said, smiling down at her. "Fifteen bucks apiece and all the beer we can drink. Right, Harry?"

"Right," Harry said. He pointed to a sign behind the bar that said LIVE ENTERTAINMENT SATURDAY NIGHT . . . THE TEXAS INSTRUMENTS . . . 9 P.M.

"Can I have the sign afterwards?" Marcie said.

Harry smiled. "Sure thing. Stick it up on your wall. Show your friends. Tell 'em about Po' Boy's."

She followed Abner and Freddie over to the small stage at the far end of the bar. There were about a dozen tables scattered around; and while Abner and Freddie set up the mikes, three couples came in and put two tables together to accommodate themselves. She tried not to think about who would be there listening when they played. She would pretend it was just another practice session at Freddie's.

She helped adjust the height of the mike she would be using and said "one-two-three" into it, feeling like an old pro. Suddenly terribly hungry, when she had a free moment she went into the tiny offstage area and ate half of her granola bar. It was dry and made her thirsty so she decided to get a glass of beer after all, to sip on and keep her mouth from drying out with nervousness. This was worse than being the valedictorian in high school!

She wasn't old enough to be drinking in a bar, but Harry didn't ask any questions and she took her glass of light back to what Abner was calling the Green Room. He seemed to be in a good mood, not high and jumpy, just relaxed and funny, the way he had been when she first met him. Freddie was very serious and intent on the PA system, but when he had it set up to his satisfaction, he came back, too, and gave her a reassuring grin.

"I hope we don't get a real rush of fans back here after the act," Abner said. "The Green Room just won't accommodate 'em."

Marcie giggled. The idea of a rush of fans was funny, and this tiny dusty room was barely big enough to hold the three of them. There were two broken chairs and a table missing a leg.

Abner gently pushed back a strand of hair that had fallen onto her forehead, and she thought of the first time she had met him, when he zipped up her bridesmaid's dress. It was hard to sort out her feelings for Abner; like knowing two different people. But right now she felt very fond of him.

Freddie looked out into the bar and signaled Harry to turn off the TV. "Pretty good crowd," he said to Marcie and Abner. "Not spectacular but pretty good. Are you ready?"

Marcie had a wild impulse to say "No!" but she followed Freddie onto the stage (which was, she thought, a fancy name for this too-small raised platform that barely held all their

121

equipment). Harry was introducing them, obviously enjoying his moment as master of ceremonies.

". . . and here they are, ladies and gentlemen, for your enjoyment, that talented little group, the Texas Instruments!"

Marcie managed a weak smile as the thin patter of applause greeted them. The faces were a blur, and there seemed to be many more of them than before.

Freddie struck a strong chord on his Martin and said, " 'Evenin', ladies and gentlemen, glad to be here with y'all" He was sounding very Texan. "We're goin' to start off tonight with that old-timey favorite, 'Foggy Mountain Breakdown.' " He struck another chord and went flying into the number.

For a terrible moment Marcie thought she was not going to be able to keep up. She threw a wild look at Abner and got a warm smile of encouragement. And then she was with them, forgetting everything except the music. She had never been able to think about anything except the music itself when she played bluegrass, and this time was no different. When she took her break, she knew it had gone well, and she was only very dimly conscious of the applause that came from the table where the three couples sat.

At the end of the number there was a good hand, no wild standing ovation, but it wasn't bad.

"Thank you very kindly," Freddie was saying. "Abner Frothingham on the banjo, Marcie Lee on guitar, and yours truly Freddie Ayers. Thank you a whole lot. We're going to play for you 'I Don't Believe You've Met My Baby.' " He glanced at Marcie and Abner and again played the strong chord with which he always started a number. Marcie swallowed. She had to sing in this one, but only in harmony.

She glanced up as some people came in, and for a moment she lost the beat. It was Kate and Aunt Meg and Manuel.

122

Kate had said they would come if Manuel could get away from some case he was working on. She was glad they were here, but for a moment it made her nervous. Then she settled into playing.

They did "Blue Ridge Mountain Home," and "John Hardy," "Can't You Hear Me Callin' You," and "Gold Rush." Marcie was happy to be playing the Gibson. It was so much easier, so much more satisfying, than her old cigar box.

They did "Duelling Banjos," with Freddie playing his mandolin. It was really Abner's and Freddie's show, that number, and they played at breakneck speed. Her job was mainly to keep up with them. It got a good hand. Kate and Aunt Meg and Manuel were clapping and stamping their feet like mad. She tossed them a kiss when the number was over, relaxing and enjoying herself now. Freddie gave her a quick hug and said, "We're takin' a short break, folks. Don't go 'way." And they went off stage to Abner's "Green Room."

The TV came back on. Marcie flopped on one of the old chairs. "Whew! That was fun!"

Abner laughed. "You're born to the business, kid."

"You're playing real good, Marcie," Freddie said. "Real good."

Someone stuck his head around the corner of the little room. It was Eric, with a bottle of Coke in his hand. "Hey, you guys, doin' good."

"Eric!" Marcie hugged him, and Freddie said, "You bring your instrument, man?"

"Nah," Freddie said. "My mother kept a hawkeye on me. I'm supposed to be over at my friend Bonnie's house doing a social call on the girl of my dreams. She'll cover for me if my mom calls up."

"Aunt Meg and Kate are out there," Marcie said.

"I know. They won't squeal. See you later." He waved and left.

"That's a good one, that Eric," Abner said.

"Damned good musician," Freddie said.

Marcie stored the comments away in her mind to tell Eric later.

The fifteen minutes went by quickly, and they filed out onto the stage again. A man at the bar, slightly drunk, complained when the TV was shut off. Marcie saw Manuel get up and go to him, put his hand on his shoulder, and speak quietly to him. The man subsided.

She was poised, ready for the opening of "Devil's Dream," the number she had practiced flat-picking on, after she had had her first lesson with Freddie. She saw some people come in. They sat down near Kate's party. It was Peg and John, Nana, and her mother. Marcie missed the opening chords altogether and came in a beat behind. She caught Freddie's anxious glance and made herself concentrate. She made it, but she was not playing her best.

At the end of the number there was a lot of applause and foot-stomping and a few encouraging yells from a trio of heavy-booted cowboy types who had come in late. Marcie avoided looking at her family. She tried not to think about them, but she couldn't completely keep them out of her mind. They were sitting right there in full view, after all. How could Peg have done that? But she knew all too well how. Her mother would have wheedled and manipulated. And Nana probably came along to keep the lid on things.

"You okay?" Freddie said out of the corner of his mouth, as he bowed and smiled to the applause.

It was a test, and she prided herself on tests. "I'm great," she said.

He shot her a look. "Thank you, thank you, folks. How 'bout 'Blackberry Blossom'?" In the midst of yells of approval, they started. Marcie saw John bring drinks from the bar to the table. She wondered what her mother was drinking. Something innocuous, certainly. Then she forgot them all. She loved "Blackberry Blossom," and she played her heart out.

They did a gospel song, "Crying Holy," and "Love, Please Come Home," a couple of Flatt and Scruggs favorites, "Never No Mo' Blues," and "Riding the Elevated Railroad."

When they stopped, the applause generated by Marcie's family and friends sparked a real ovation. There was clapping and stomping and yells of "More!"

They played "Dear Old Sunny South by the Sea" and made their exit to the offstage room.

But the applause went on.

After a minute, Freddie said, "This is unreal." But he was grinning with pleasure. "It's your kinfolks, Marcie."

"Let's give the public what they want," Abner said. "How about 'Sally Goodin'?"

They went back out, to whistles and stomps and rebel yells, and played "Sally Goodin'."

Marcie saw Aunt Meg get to her feet, with Eric only a second behind her, then Kate and Manuel, Peg, John, and Nana. She heard Nana's New England equivalent of a rebel yell. But her mother sat like a stony statue, not clapping, not smiling, not moving. Damn her, Marcie thought, damn her, damn her, damn her. She felt the tears streaming down her face, and she didn't know whether they were for joy or anger. She *had* been good, she knew she had; she had never played better. Why couldn't her mother . . . Oh, why couldn't she . . . She rushed offstage.

Abner and Freddie followed more slowly. Freddie said,

"Was that your mother?" and when she nodded, he gave her a hard hug.

"You could have fooled me," Abner said. "I thought it was the Great Stone Face."

"Shut up, Ab," Freddie said.

"It's all right." Marcie mopped her face. "I apologize for her. But otherwise, it was great, wasn't it?"

"You outdid yourself," Freddie said ."I didn't know you could play that good. Yet. And you'll just get better and better because you're one hell of a quick learner and you *work*."

She knew he was trying to cheer her up, but she was also sure he wouldn't say she was good unless he thought so. "I owe it all to my sainted teacher," she said, trying to grin. She took a deep breath. "Well, let's go collect our free beer."

She stopped at the bar to return her half full, now warm and flat beer and to get something cold. Her throat was dry, and she felt shaky. "Make it a Coke instead, will you, Harry?"

Several of the men sitting at the bar told her they'd liked her music. One of the cowboy types leaned against the bar, his faded denim legs crossed and his scruffy boots in everybody's way. His old Stetson was shoved onto the back of his head. In a loud voice that carried across the room, he said, "You done real good, little lady. Played like a damn angel. Didn't know a girl could do that."

She smiled, biting her tongue on the retort she felt like making. Girl, indeed! But she knew he meant to compliment her.

People were moving around, getting fresh drinks now that the music was over. It took her a minute to make her way to her family. Manuel and John had moved their tables together earlier. As she got nearer to them, she saw her mother's back as she went out the door. John, following her, looked back with a helpless gesture, then he too was gone. Peg looked as if she would explode. Nana's smile was strained.

Manuel and Eric jumped up and both of them hugged Marcie. Then everybody was hugging her at once. Aunt Meg was saying, "Honey, you played like a Texan!"

Eric said, "I never knew you were that good."

Manuel pulled out the chair her mother had been in, and she sat down.

"Well," Peg said, "don't blame me. She told me you expected us. I'm sorry. I should have known it was one of her tricks."

"Let's forget it," Nana said. "It was wonderful, and we're going to have a wonderful evening. Marian never hurts anyone as much as she hurts herself. Darling, I am so *proud* of you!"

"Did you like it, Jane?" Marcie grinned at Peg's look of shock. "She wants us to call her Jane." She leaned over and kissed her sister's cheek. "Stop looking tragic. It's wonderful to see you. Did you have a super honeymoon?"

Peg's face relaxed. "Wonderful! Listen, John is coming right back, as soon as he dumps you-know-who. Nana wants to take us all out for supper somewhere."

"I fought her for the privilege," Aunt Meg said, "but your Jane won."

"She usually does," Marcie said. "Luckily for all of us." She was feeling happy now. She wasn't going to think about her mother.

"Your fellow-minstrels also," Nana said. "Can you lure them away from the bar?"

"Sure." Marcie stood up and caught Freddie's eye. She

127

gestured, and he and Abner came over to the table. "Fellow minstrels," she said, "this groupie here is my grandmother, Jane. I guess you know everybody else."

"We want you to join us for supper," Nana said. "As soon as John comes back. Please do. You were wonderful. My head rings. In a nice way, of course."

Much, much later, after one of the happiest evenings Marcie could remember having, she stood outside her apartment house saying goodnight to John and Peg, who had followed her home. "What exactly was Mom's problem, aside from the fact that it wasn't the Waldorf Astoria?"

"Well, that was basically it. She saw it as an evil dive or something. She thinks the next step in your downward path is probably prostitution. 'Everybody knows,' she said, 'what kind of life a bar girl leads.' "

"Personally," John said, "I think she's mad because you're so good. She hoped you'd flop and go on home like a dutiful daughter. Listen, Marcie, you stick around as long as you want to—forever, I hope—and don't forget we're on your side, two hundred percent. I mean anything we can do—I mean *anything* . . . Consider it done."

Marcie reached across Peg and grabbed his hand. "I may have lost a mother, but look at the brother I got." She gave Peg a quick kiss and ran into the house.

In her apartment the phone was ringing.

128

# 22

The phone had stopped ringing before she got to it, and she let it go. It had to be her mother. Who else, at this ungodly hour. And a conversation with her mother was the last thing she wanted. She unplugged the phone, brushed her teeth, fell into bed, and slept till noon the next day.

She was drinking her coffee when the special delivery came. On Hotel Driskill stationery.

Dear Marcie, (her mother wrote)

I have tried and tried to call you, but you do not seem to be there. I'd rather not think where you might be. I have talked to your father, and he agrees with me that you should come home. You are obviously not mature enough to be out on your own yet. Last night's

129

performance in that disgusting place made that clear to me. We called them B-girls in my day. I don't know what you call them now, but it adds up to the same thing. I have bought two plane tickets for Boston for Monday, nine twenty a.m. We'll see about having your car driven north. There are people who do that for a fee. Please call me WHEN YOU COME BACK to that place you're living.

*Your loving Mother.*

Marcie read it over twice, and then she plugged in her phone and dialed her father. She didn't even bother to say hello when he answered. "Why did you tell Mother that I have to go home? You could at least have discussed it with me."

There was a pause. "Would you say that again?" he said.

She said it again.

"Marcie, listen to me, and listen good. I wouldn't do a thing like that, and you ought to know it. Your mother called me at two a.m., woke me out of a sound sleep, told me some hysterical tale about you playing with a couple of hippies in a cheap dive where everybody was high on dope and cowboys were making passes at you. She said I had to cut off your money. I said I didn't think so. I hung up and tried to call you and got a busy signal. I tried again this morning. Now what in hell is going on?"

She let her breath out in a long whoosh. "Dad, I'm sorry. I just got this special delivery from Mom, and I was so mad, I couldn't think. I'm sorry. I should have known. Mom wangled Peg into taking her to hear me play last night. I wrote you about our gig, our first one—"

"How'd it go?" He sounded eager now.

"Like a dream. Wonderful. Of course, most of the applause came from my friends and relatives. Except Mom, who sat there like a rock and never even clapped. She left before I could get out there afterward. Made John take her home. It's true, it was just a little dingy bar, a workingman's hangout, but there's nothing wrong with it, and anyway Freddie would kill anybody that bothered me—"

"Listen, you don't have to explain. I know you, after all. You always had good sense. Your mother is making last-ditch efforts to make you come home. All I can say is, if you give in, I really will cut you off, from college and everything else. Hang in there, Marcie. I love you, I trust you. Your mother is a sick woman. I've been telling her for years she ought to see a shrink, but she's insulted, furious, when I mention it. Look, sweetie, is your grandmother still there?"

"Yes."

"Talk to her. And hang on. I love you."

She put the phone back and sat thinking. She didn't really want to drag Nana into this if she didn't have to. She had to handle this herself.

The phone rang, and her stomach clenched. But it was Freddie.

"How ya doin'? Me, I'm hung over from all that good food. That grandmother of yours is a marvel."

"It was a wonderful night. Except for the fly in the ointment." She told him about her letter and her phone call to her father.

"Well, I don't know if you want advice or not, but I'll give it. Do nothing."

"Nothing?"

"Nothing. Ignore it."

"But somebody may come and pick up my car. And she's got a plane ticket for me."

131

"So let her cash it in. Anyway we've got plans for next weekend."

"We have? Another gig?"

"No, there's a bluegrass festival in Galveston. Abner just heard about it. We think we should go. Eric wants to go, too. We can hear a lot of good stuff, and maybe play a little pickup in the parking lot or whatever. It'll do you good to hear some top-drawer music."

"I'd love it."

"Okay, we'll plan on it. Take a couple days off now, not from practicing but from lessons. And I'll see you Tuesday, same time."

After he hung up, she had another cup of coffee and tried to think what to do. She couldn't entirely do nothing, but she was not about to get into any big scene with her mother. They never got her anywhere. So she decided to use her mother's method. She found some stationery that she had bought to write to Vin and her friends at home. It took three rough drafts before she got one that seemed to do.

Dear Mother,

I'm sorry you couldn't reach me. I was out with Nana and Peg and my friends. Everyone but you seemed to enjoy our music. I'm sorry you didn't. I have talked to Dad. I think you misunderstood him. Anyway I am staying here. As soon as you get home, you'll feel better, with your friends around you. I'll try to come home for Christmas. Let's don't be angry with each other.

I do love you, you know.

*Marcie.*

She dressed and drove to the nearest postal station to mail it, then changed her mind and dropped it off at the desk of the

Driskill. It was crazy, having to communicate with your mother by mail when she was right there. But Marcie knew if she went up to see her, she would never get a chance to explain herself. They would both lose their tempers, her mother would cry, and Marcie would feel like a monster for making her mother so unhappy.

On the way home she stopped to see Kate. She had to talk to somebody, and Peg wouldn't do; she'd just get upset. Kate wasn't involved.

Kate let her talk, asked a few questions, persuaded her to stay for lunch. It felt good to let it all out, although sometimes when she was trying to put it into words, it sounded so absurd, so childish, as if she and her mother were two little kids trying to one-up each other. She said that to Kate.

"Well," Kate said, "it seems to me you and your mother are locked in a kind of waltz, with all the predictable steps. She's a charming woman, when she wants to be, though she's never tried hard to charm me."

"I never understood why she didn't like you."

"I suppose she blamed me for Peg's never going home."

"But she and Peg do nothing but fight when they're together."

"Maybe that's another duet. Peg is pretty guilt-ridden too, you know. She just has a different set of reactions. Flight, for one. What kind of relationship does your mother have with her mother?"

"They don't understand each other at all. Mom says Nana never wanted to have a child, but I don't think that's true."

"But if she thinks it, it's true for her. If you dug around, you'd probably find some kind of insecurity that your grandmother felt with her own mother."

"Oh, I don't think so. Nana is so sane."

"Maybe because she came to terms with it. Your mother didn't."

Marcie was silent for several minutes. "You're saying I'd better learn how to come to terms with it."

"No, I'm not telling you what to do. It's your waltz. You're the only one who can stop the music. And it won't be easy. We all have this little kid in us who doesn't want to grow up and take charge."

"Not you."

"Oh yes, me." She paused. "Speaking of which . . . I have some news. Nobody knows it yet except my parents. I talked to them in London last night." She was smiling, and Marcie thought she had never seen her look so radiant.

"What is it?"

"Manuel and I are going to get married."

"Kate! That's wonderful! I'm so glad. When?"

"Quick, before I lose my nerve. It still doesn't seem right to subject Manuel to such a risk, but he won't let up. He called Father Steve this morning and set a date so I couldn't back out. It's Friday."

"*This* Friday?"

Kate grinned. "This very Friday. We'll get married at the church and have a very small 'do' at Aunt Meg's, just like Peg's, only we aren't having any people except half a dozen kinfolks and you."

"I'm glad you asked me. I couldn't have stood it not to come."

"Of course we'd have you. You're kinfolks now, too. Will you bring your guitar? Would you mind?"

"I'd love to."

"Good." Kate looked out the window for a long moment. "It's a big risk."

"I guess everybody's at risk one way or another."

"I guess. Mine happens to be a little more obvious than most." She smiled. "But I must say, I can't wait to take it."

"You've made my day," Marcie said. "In more ways than one."

# 23

The next morning Marcie called her mother. She had been thinking a lot about what Kate had said. It was true, she did fall into a pattern, a "waltz," as Kate called it. Her mother complained and she reacted with guilt and tried to please; or as she'd been doing lately, she rebelled and her mother was angry and she still reacted with guilt. It was time to change the tape, though she wasn't sure just how to go about it.

"Good morning," her mother said. She sounded a bit cool, but after a minute she chatted as if nothing had happened. She didn't mention the exchange of letters. It was the "pretend it never happened" ploy. She didn't refer to the gig either. Instead, she told Marcie about a woman she had gotten

136

acquainted with in the Driskill restaurant. Mrs. Duplessis. "A lovely woman, from Charleston, South Carolina. She's one of the Ravenels."

"What's a Ravenel?" Marcie asked.

"Oh, Marcie. The Ravenels are one of the first families of Charleston. Terribly distinguished."

"Oh." Marcie was willing to bet that her mother had never heard of them before either. "Did she tell you that? Did she sit down for coffee and say, 'Hey, I'm a Ravenel?' " Marcie was trying to be funny. It usually worked, because her mother had a good sense of the ridiculous when she wasn't busy being offended or martyred or something.

She laughed. "No, honey, it just came out in the conversation. She has a lovely accent, very southern and aristocratic."

Marcie wanted to ask why a South Carolina accent was okay, but a Texas accent wasn't, but she was smart enough not to say that. Not today, when she was trying to be grownup-to-grownup. "How are you feeling? How's your ear?"

"As a matter of fact, I'm having a lot of trouble with it." Her voice took on the faint whine of complaint that was so familiar. "Mrs. Duplessis told me about a wonderful doctor in Houston. I'm going to call and make an appointment."

"Oh." Marcie really didn't want to change the tone of this conversation, which so far was pleasant, but she couldn't go on as if there were nothing to talk about. "Will you fly home from Houston then? You might be able to get a direct flight from there and avoid Dallas–Forth Worth."

There was a long silence.

"Mom? Are you still there?"

"I was thinking," her mother said, "that you would drive me to Houston."

For a wild moment Marcie wanted to say, "You could ride on Abner's motorcycle when we go to Galveston." But instead she said, "It's a three or four hour drive, I think. That would be eight hours if you came back here. It seems unnecessarily tiring for you."

"And inconvenient for you?" Her mother's tone was not chatty and pleasant now.

"As a matter of fact, I've got a busy week." She wasn't about to tell her about Kate's marriage or about the music festival either. She fought down the impulse to apologize for having plans. "But I can get your ticket and all that, if you want."

"Oh, I wouldn't think of bothering you."

"Come on, Mom, don't be like that." She kept her voice quiet. "You know I'll do whatever I can. But I can't devote my life . . ." That wasn't coming out right.

"To me? No, of course not. I devoted mine to you, but, as Shakespeare said, 'sharper than a serpent's tooth,' and so on."

"Look, why don't we have lunch? We can't get anywhere on the phone." She didn't want to take the time for lunch. She had a lesson with Freddie tonight and a lot of practicing to do. But maybe it was the least she could do.

"I wouldn't think of interfering with your life," her mother said, and hung up.

Marcie leaned back in the chair. "Shit," she said, knowing she was dancing to Mom's tune, just the way she always did. She felt guilty in the same old way. How did you beat this rap? She got up and went into the kitchen and made some instant coffee. Instant solutions. Maybe there weren't any. One slow step at a time. See Mom's point of view, but don't give in to her. She tried to think about Mom as a kid, thinking Nana didn't want her. Had Nana really not wanted her? They had never seemed fond of each other. Nana said she never understood her. So Mom has this hangup of not being wanted, and she takes it out on her own kids. And Mom always had a thing about not being pretty. Nana was beautiful when she was young; Marcie had seen pictures. She was still pretty. That would matter, maybe, to a kid who felt insecure to begin with.

She really tried to project herself into the role of her mother as a child, but it was hard to do. Partly because she loved Nana so much. If she had kids, would she ruin their lives too? No, wait a minute. The kid's life wouldn't be ruined if the kid refused to let it be.

She finished her coffee and got her guitar. She couldn't sit around thinking in circles forever. She wanted to try that banjo–mandolin piece with Freddie, only with guitar–mandolin. It was tricky. One instrument played a phrase and the other one repeated it, very fast, all through the number. Kind of like "Anything You Can Do, I Can Do Better."

While she was practicing, she could forget about her mother and everything else.

Later in the afternoon Peg called to give her the big news about Kate and Manuel. Marcie didn't say she already knew. It would spoil Peg's pleasure in telling her.

"And have you talked to Nana lately? She and Bridget are planning a trip to Argentina. Isn't she the one!"

Marcie was glad of that for several reasons. If Nana were gone, it would be one less reason for Mom to hang around. Not that they saw each other much, she'd gathered. But it seemed to be kind of a competition with Mom: if Nana could stay in Austin, so could she.

"Come have dinner with us tomorrow night," Peg went on. "We ought to think of something fun to do about the wedding.

It's coming up so fast. But that's good; Kate won't have time to change her mind."

"I'd love to, unless we have practice. I can tell you in the morning." She told Peg about the Galveston trip. "Don't tell Mom. She'll think I'm being kidnapped, white slavery or something."

"Don't worry. I tell her nothing."

She hung up thinking what a good week it was turning out to be. Dinner with Peg and John, Kate's marriage, Galveston. Nothing as interesting as any of those things would happen to her in a month at home.

Abner didn't show up for practice, but that was not unusual. He came when the spirit moved him. She and Freddie played for a long time and then sat around talking.

"Let her go to Houston," he said, about her mother. "Maybe she'll meet an oil millionaire. Hasn't she ever thought about getting married again?"

"I think she'd be scared to. Several guys have come around from time to time, and she enjoys that, but she doesn't let herself get serious. Once burned, I guess."

He tipped up his bottle of Dos Equis and drained it. "Want another lemonade?" He had found out that she loved lemonade, and now he made it fresh for her every time she came. "My ex is getting married again. Celebration. No more alimony payments."

"That's good. Do you still . . . uh . . . feel emotional about her?"

"Not often. I guess you never get totally unattached from anyone you've been attached to. She's a good person. Only she wants a young executive type, and this time she's getting one."

"How boring."

"Don't knock it. It's security."

"Security. Why does everybody get so hung up about security? Nothing's really secure anyway."

"True. But money in the bank is something some people can get fond of. Like me; I could."

"Not me."

"That's because you've got an old man that's got it. You don't know what it feels like to be cold, stony broke."

Marcie thought about that on the way home. He was right. She had never had to think about where the next meal was coming from. It could make a difference. She thought of something she had had on her mind before; she wanted to ask Manuel if he could use office help. He worked so much of the time for people who had no money, she knew he operated on a shoestring. She could type and stuff envelopes and do it for free and learn something about the world. She'd ask him.

# 24

There had been a tense moment when Abner asked, "Who's going to ride with who?" He was taking his motorcycle to Galveston, and Freddy was taking his van, which would also carry the instruments.

"I'd give an arm and a leg to ride with you," Eric said, "as long as my mother doesn't find out. She thinks I'm going to a nice, quiet music festival with nice, quiet Freddie."

"Well, don't look at me," Freddie said. "Who do you want to ride with, Marcie?"

Marcie hesitated and saw Abner start to turn away. He was expecting her to refuse. She had not been alone with him since the episode in Freddie's yard. "I'll go with Abner if nobody minds," she said. Seeing Eric's look of disappointment, she added, "Maybe we could swap around coming home."

She was waiting now for Abner to pick her up. As far as she knew, Freddie and Eric were already on their way. She thought about Kate and Manuel. It had been her idea of a perfect way to get married, the simple ceremony at church and then the informal get-together at Aunt Meg's with just sixteen people. Uncle Joe had showed up for the church service, but he took off afterward. John had given Kate away, and Peg had stood up with Kate. They were going to take just the weekend for a honeymoon because Manuel had to appear in court Monday with one of his clients. Marcie was sure all of them had been crossing their fingers that Kate would live a long time and have a happy life with Manuel, so there was a touch of sadness that was different from Peg's wedding. And yet who could tell what might happen to anybody.

Her mother had been annoyed at not being invited to the wedding, even though both Peg and Marcie had tried to make her understand that it was a small family affair. Marcie knew her mother didn't really want to go; she just wanted to be asked. She had tried to pressure Marcie into having dinner tonight with her and her new friend, Mrs. Duplessis. Marcie had explained that she was going to a music festival "somewhere south of here, in the country," but she had finally agreed to a late dinner Sunday night. She knew she'd be tired and probably just barely back from Galveston, but she gave in.

"Your grandmother is in town for the moment," her mother said. "She flits in and out like a pigeon, but she says she wants to talk to me. We're going to church Sunday together. I don't know what's on her mind."

Marcie too wondered what Nana wanted to talk to her

mother about. She suspected it might be an attempt to get her to go home.

She looked out the window and saw Abner coming around the corner in one of his big swooping turns, and at the same moment that she saw it, she heard the BMW. She grabbed her backpack and went down to meet him. Freddie was taking the Gibson for her.

"Am I late?" He looked happy. "We've got a good day for it. Look, I got a special new lambskin seat for you."

"That's great, but you didn't have to do that."

"It's a long ride to Galveston, friend. You'll be glad that little lamb sacrificed his hide for you." He waited while she got settled. "There's a hurricane brewing in the Caribbean. Cross your fingers that it stays away from Galveston. I was there once in a hurricane, and it's wild."

"Consider them crossed." But it was hard to think of bad weather on such a perfect day. The weather had cooled off some, there was a fresh breeze and a blue sky. Good motor-cycle-riding weather, she thought, as she adjusted the helmet and got her shoulder pack comfortable. "Anchors aweigh, my lad."

He turned his head and gave her a flashing smile. "Righto, Cap." And they were off with a roar and a swoop.

In no time at all they were out of town and heading toward Houston and Galveston. She was excited about seeing the Gulf, and about the festival, and about life in general. It really was a kick, riding on the motorcycle. She was glad she wasn't in the van. Coming home, though, she'd better let Eric ride the motorcycle. She knew he was aching to.

They stopped in a small town for a cup of coffee, about two hours later, and in Houston they had lunch. Marcie insisted on paying for it. "I'm getting a free ride, after all."

Abner was in the best of moods. He talked a lot and made her laugh. She wondered for a moment what he did for a living. She had asked Freddie once, and he had said, "Who knows? A job here, a deal there. Maybe it's just as well not to ask." She wondered if that buccaneer quality of Abner's was one of the things that made him attractive. She had to remind herself now and then not to find him too attractive. That other Abner, in the yard at Freddie's, seemed like someone else. But he wasn't. It was all one Abner.

It was late in the afternoon when they got to Galveston. The view of the Gulf as they crossed from the mainland to the island made her suddenly homesick. This water was more intensely blue than her North Atlantic, but it was good to see ocean again.

Abner took her on a quick tour of the town and then headed out toward the festival, which was in a field not far from the tiny airport. On the festival grounds there were several big striped tents. The sounds of music came at them even before Abner shut off the BMW motor. They saw Freddie's van in the parking lot, but Freddie and Eric weren't there. Marcie was tingling with excitement. The sky was clouding up, but with the tents it wouldn't make all that much difference even if it did rain.

In the parking lot, and scattered around in the field, impromptu groups were playing. She and Abner wandered around, half looking for Freddie, but mostly just seeing what was here. When Abner stopped to talk to some people he knew, she went on by herself smiling broadly. People smiled back and said, "Howdy." It was different from the festival in New Orleans, less concentrated. But when she went into the biggest of the tents, she realized that the serious action was as good, if not better. A group called Town Limits Bluegrass

Band was going all out on the stage at the far end of the tent. There were a lot of people listening, but she found a place to sit on the grass with the canvas at her back.

She was still sitting there, when Freddie and Eric found her. Another group had just finished to big applause, and the master of ceremonies was talking about a new group that was about to play.

"Aren't you hungry?" Eric said.

She looked at her watch and was amazed to see how late it was. Freddie gave her a hand up, and they went out to the van, where he had a styrofoam cooler full of beer and lemon-ade and sandwiches, potato chips, Doritos, and cheese. Marcie discovered that she was starving.

The sky had darkened, and a light rain had begun, but no one was paying much attention, beyond making sure their instruments didn't get wet. Eric found Abner, and she and Eric sat in the front of the van, Abner and Freddie sprawled out in the back, eating and comparing notes on what they had heard.

They had brought sleeping bags, and the plan had been for Marcie to sleep in the back of the van, Eric on the front seat, Abner and Freddie in their sleeping bags outside the van. The rain, however, was prompting a change. It was finally decided that if it kept up, Freddie would drive Marcie to a motel, and the other three would sleep inside the van. With the instru-ments, there would be just barely enough room.

"You're looking shiny-eyed," Freddie said to Marcie. "Glad you came, rain and all?"

"Oh, yes! You know I am."

"How come," Eric said, "a born-and-bred Yankee like you goes for bluegrass so big?"

Marcie tried to think how to answer that. She wasn't sure.

"I'll tell you why," Abner said. "What's characteristic of bluegrass! It's fresh and lively and honest and more fun than, as my sainted grandmother used to say, a barrel full of monkeys. And you could say those same things to describe Marcie, right?"

Eric thought about it and nodded.

Marcie was touched, but she answered lightly. "I like that barrel full of monkeys."

"That was my North Carolina grandmother. She had some expressions even the Texans can't match."

Freddie stretched. "Well, let's get back and hear some music. I guess we can't set up any little pickups of our own, 'cause there's no place to do it but out in the rain." He locked the van and they went back to one of the other tents, where a group from New Mexico were playing their hearts out.

The rain was coming down harder now, seeping in under the canvas, and the tent itself was billowing and flapping in the increasing wind. Marcie thought of the hurricane in the Caribbean and then forgot about it. She had never been in a hurricane or a tornado, so she found it hard to think about them as something real.

Around midnight, things began to die down. Cars and pickups and vans moved out of the parking area. A couple of them got stuck in the gumbolike mud that the rain was creating.

Marcie and the others piled into the van, after Abner checked the BMW and moved it to higher ground. The wheels spun as Freddie tried to get started, but he gunned the motor and got out. The wind was blowing hard.

They took Marcie to a motel to check in, and then the

four of them went downtown to find a place to eat. There was a small restaurant still open facing the beach. Marcie had Texas chicken fried steak and gravy for the first time in her life and was surprised to find that she liked it.

Rain beat against the restaurant windows, and a man went outside to let down a metal awning that shielded the front of the place. "Blowin' up a gale," he said when he came in. His shirt was soaked and his hair plastered to his head.

"Think it'll blow over by morning?" Freddie asked him.

He shrugged. "You never know around here. Sometimes she hits hard, sometimes she blows right by us."

"I wonder," Freddie said when the man had gone into the back of the restaurant, "if we ought to take off for home tonight."

"Not me," Abner said. "I'm not driving the BMW in this rain. Wouldn't be able to see a foot."

"Oh, it'll be clear by morning," Eric said. "And think of all we'd miss. I mean we've come all this way. I specially want to hear that bunch from West Texas. I've heard they're real good."

Freddie looked at Marcie. "What do you say?"

"I say stay."

He rubbed his hand over his beard. "All right. But I'll put the radio on in the van from time to time, and if it sounds bad, we'll come pick you up. So if somebody hammers on your door at a peculiar hour, it's only us."

After they left her, Marcie lay awake a little while. She was still going over the music in her head, and behind it were the swish and slash of rain against her window and across the road the pounding of the surf. She went to sleep feeling good.

# 25

Someone was pounding on her door. It was pitch dark, and the rain was coming down like thunder. The motel shook in the wind, and outside Marcie could hear objects blowing and smashing into things. It sounded as if a box factory had suddenly dumped all its boxes and tools into the street. And above the other sounds came the smash-and-withdraw, smash-and-withdraw of the surf.

Marcie grabbed her sweat shirt, pulled it over her pajamas, and opened the door. Freddie was there, dripping rain from his hair and his beard. His T-shirt clung to his broad chest. "We're getting out," he said. "Grab your stuff. I've got the van right out here." The force of the wind made him grab the door. Inside the room a picture of palm trees banged against

149

the wall, tore loose, and crashed to the floor in a mess of broken glass.

"Two seconds." Marcie had to lean against the door to close it. She pulled on her jeans over her pajama pants, got on her Adidas, and crammed everything else into her shoulder pack.

Freddie was waiting just outside the door. He grabbed her arm; they bent over and ran for the van. Eric opened the door as he saw them coming. Abner was waiting with his motorcycle in the slight protection from the wind that the van offered.

People were coming out of their rooms and driving off in a hurry. Already the road along the shore was bumper-to-bumper cars. Horns blew, lights flared.

Freddie and Abner got the rear doors of the van open and lifted the heavy motorcycle inside. Abner climbed in and sat beside it. Eric had already moved the instruments forward to make room, and he was curled up just behind the driver's seat.

The van rocked in the wind as Freddie drove out of the parking lot and waited for a break that would let him into the flow of traffic. Debris blew past them, a trashcan spilling trash as it rolled end over end, sand beating against the windshield with the rain. Across the road a big tree began to fall as if in slow motion, pulling against the anchor of its roots. The van seemed to leap forward as Freddie floored the gas pedal. The tree fell as they passed, its branches scraping against the back of the van.

"Whew!" Eric said. "Look, that tree is stopping the traffic behind us."

Nobody answered. Freddie was bent forward trying to see

150

through the deluge of rain on his windshield. The windshield wipers strained and pushed at the curtain of water but they were ineffectual. Freddie rolled down his window part way and stuck his head out to see what was ahead, but in a minute he closed the window again, his face streaked with rain. The van swayed dangerously.

It was a relief to turn off Seawall Boulevard, but the two-mile-long Causeway to the mainland was not going to be easy either. A fire engine screamed past them, going the other way. Marcie saw a man standing on the porch of a small frame house, holding his arm up to ward off the rain. As she watched, a door flew through the air and smashed into the side of the house. The man leaped off the steps. And then she couldn't see them any more.

The water was sloshing across the Causeway, washing up over the wheels of the cars. The station wagon in front of Freddie stalled, and without slackening speed he cut around it. Marcie saw the look of anguish on the driver's face as they passed him. He was fighting to get the car started again.

A little further on a small foreign car in front of the van was blown sideways across the Causeway, as if it were made of paper. Its left wheels dangled dangerously off the road. Freddie slowed. The young woman who had been in the car alone crawled out the passenger door.

"Get her in, Eric," Freddie said.

Eric slid the panel door partway open and yelled. She struggled to the car and grabbed his hand, running alongside. Abner reached out to help, and the two of them pulled her headfirst into the van. Freddie speeded up.

"My God!" the woman said. She was white as a sheet and trembling. "Thanks." She was breathing hard.

"Don't thank us too soon," Abner said. "We're not out of this mess yet."

The woman huddled against the side of the van in the only available space. Eric was sitting on some of the sleeping bags, and every time the van hit debris in the road, he cracked his head against the roof.

No one spoke as Freddie fought the wind that tried to push him off the road. Twice he cut around stalled cars. Someone in one of them got out and was immediately blown flat on the ground. Freddie had to swerve not to hit him. He looked in the rearview mirror. "The car behind us is picking him up."

They were halfway across the Causeway, about a mile left to go, when the van stalled. Freddie cursed under his breath and tried to start it. Nothing happened. Cars cut around him and went on. The van, stationery, caught the force of the wind harder than ever. It shook and seemed about to tip over.

"I'm taking the BMW out," Abner said, in a quick, firm voice that Marcie hadn't heard before. "I can take the women, and I'll come back for you and Eric. Don't start walking. You're better off in the van, unless it starts to slide into the water." He had the back panel door open, and Eric was helping him with the motorcycle.

"It's dangerous," Freddie said. "You'll get blown away."

"I don't think so. We're low to the ground, and I can go a lot faster than cars. I can cut around 'em. Come on, Marcie, and you, sister. Hurry it up. The water's getting deeper by the second."

The two women crowded onto the seat, Marcie just behind Abner. Fortunately the stranger was small and thin. She wrapped her arms around Marcie's waist. "See ya." Abner waved to Freddie and Eric.

The last thing Marcie saw as they drove away was Eric's white, tight-lipped face. She should have made him go instead of her. But there would have been an argument, and there wasn't time. She was scared. If anything happened to either Eric or Freddie . . . She didn't let herself go on with the thought.

Abner was driving very fast. The water splashed up around their legs, and they had to lean forward against the wind. The motorcycle skidded wildly every now and then, and once they were blown close to the edge of the road. But Abner was able to cut around cars and make good time most of the way.

It was hard to breathe. Marcie buried her face against Abner's shoulder and kept her eyes closed.

Once they were across the bay the wind seemed not quite so fierce .A lot of junk was blowing around and trees were uprooted here and there, but the motorcycle stayed under control.

Abner turned into a farm that had a stone barn. He slewed in the mud of the barnyard and came to a stop. "Off," he said, and ran to the closed doors, struggled to open them. Marcie slogged through the ankle-deep mud to help him. There was no one in the barn except several cows in stanchions and a goat who was tethered. "Stay here," Abner said. "Be right back."

As Marcie and the other woman fought to close the barn door, she watched Abner ride at top speed back to the Causeway. She found herself praying that all three of them would get back.

They got the door closed and instantly the storm seemed far away. It was so still in the barn, they could hear the shuffle of the cows' feet on the straw. The goat watched them intently, and Marcie thought of the goat at Aunt Meg's. What was his name? It bothered her that she couldn't remember.

"I'm Marcie Lee," she said. "We were in Galveston for the music festival. We're from Austin."

The girl, who looked younger than Marcie had at first thought, was shivering, although it was warm in the barn. "Annie Guardino," she said. "Houston. I was visiting my mother. She wouldn't leave. I don't know if she's all right. She made me leave."

"She'll be all right," Marcie said, wondering why one says such fatuous things.

But Annie looked a little relieved, as if Marcie really knew. "Her house is on Twenty-fourth Street, near Ashton Villa."

Marcie remembered that Abner had pointed out Ashton Villa, a restored Italian-type villa. He'd said it was a museum now and had a Victorian dollhouse. "That sounds like a safe part of town."

"It's always been okay. Mom thought I could get out of town ahead of the traffic. She didn't realize . . . I wish I could call her up."

"The guys will be back soon." She hoped. If they couldn't get the van going . . .

As if reading her mind, Annie said, "They'll never get that van started."

All the instruments, Marcie thought. The Martin guitar. The Gibson. But never mind all that. Just get the guys through safely. "We can rent a car in Texas City or some-place," Marcie said, hoping she sounded confident, "And can drop you off in Houston."

The girl didn't answer, and Marcie suddenly felt like shaking her. She was sitting there looking totally defeated, as if

154

she didn't expect Abner and Freddie and Eric to show up at all. Marcie got up and went over to stroke the cows' noses. They looked at her with mild curiosity and didn't seem nervous. The horse she used to ride always got terribly nervous when the wind blew hard. Old Brownie. A bundle of apprehensions.

The wind whistled around the barn and the small windows rattled, but the building was firm as a rock. Well, it *was* rock. Something to be said for building on rock, not on sand. She wished she could relax. She spoke to the goat, and he grabbed her sleeve and started chewing.

"Hey, cut that out." She pulled her arm away from him. The goat gave her a comical stare. She'd never had much to do with goats. This one looked very bright, very knowing. She wondered who owned this farm. No one seemed to be around, unless they were holed up in their cellar or somewhere. Maybe they'd moved inland to get away from the storm.

She was trying not to keep looking at her watch. Time seemed to creep. But suddenly she was aware that someone was trying to open the barn door. She ran to help, her heart leaping up with relief, though maybe it was only the man who owned this place. Maybe he'd throw them out.

The door slid open, and Freddie and Eric almost tumbled into the barn. Freddie had a gash on his forehead that was bleeding. Abner was wheeling the BMW into the barn, and then the three of them got the door shut. In the stillness of the barn they looked at each other.

"We made it," Eric said in a strangled voice. He sounded like someone who has been swimming too long under water.

All three of them were drenched, and little rills of water ran along the dirt floor where they stood.

Impulsively Marcie threw her arms around Freddie. "I was so scared." Then she hugged Eric, and finally Abner. "You're a hero," she said. And when he laughed a tired little laugh, she said, "I mean it. That took courage."

"Who's got a clean handkerchief?" Abner said. "Freddie boy is bleeding like a stuck pig."

Annie Guardino surprisingly produced a large clean men's handkerchief, monogrammed. "It's my boyfriend's. But he won't care. You saved my life after all."

Freddie pressed it to his head, sitting crosslegged on the floor. In a little while the bleeding stopped. Abner was lying flat on his back on the straw of an empty stall. He looked exhausted.

"It's letting up," Marcie said, peering out the small window. "It's not raining so hard, and the wind is letting up."

"Well," Freddie said, "we need wheels. I'll try to salvage the van later, but there's no point going back into that mess now. Probably wouldn't let me anyway. There were cops all over the place when Ab came back for us."

Without opening his eyes Abner said, "I went like mad and pretended not to see 'em signaling me to stop."

"So," Freddie went on, in his slow, considering way, "I guess the only thing we can do is rent a car and get you guys home before your mothers start dragneting the countryside."

"My mother doesn't know I'm here," Marcie said.

"Mine does," Eric said. "She's probably on the hot line already."

"You can call her up when we get out of here. Ab, can I use the BMW to go into Texas City and get us a car?"

"I don't care. Just don't wreck it."

"I'll go with you," Marcie said. The barn, which had

seemed such a refuge, was beginning to make her claustro-phobic. Besides, she had that date with her mother tonight, and she needed to get home.

"Okay, let's go." The gash on Freddie's head still looked red and ugly, but it had stopped bleeding. He threw the handkerchief into a trash barrel. "Tell your boyfriend I owe him."

"He won't even miss it," Annie said. "He dresses real elegant. He works for the newspaper."

"Then you can give him a close-up picture of the hurricane."

Marcie followed Freddie out as he wheeled the BMW through the door. The rain had almost stopped, although there was still a brisk wind. Trees were down, and there was debris all over. It was probably a whole lot worse on Galveston island, she thought.

It took Freddie a minute to get the BMW started, but then they were on their way. He drove more carefully than Abner usually did, partly because it was impossible to be sure that there wouldn't be unexpected obstructions. They saw a small house with the roof blown off and a barn that was demolished. Rakes and hoes and other small farm implements were strewn on the ground and in the road, and everywhere there were limbs from trees, sometimes whole trees. Once they made a wide detour around a blown-down telephone wire. The telephone crews were out looking for trouble.

Freddie's back seemed about twice as wide as Abner's. She was thinking how dependable he was, when suddenly the bike hit a puddle of spilled oil and went into a skid. Freddie fought to control it, but the heavy BMW slid sideways toward a ditch, hit a half-smashed wooden crate, and flipped over.

Marcie felt a sharp pain in her ankle. The rear wheel was

resting on it. If she lay perfectly still, it didn't hurt, but when she tried to move out from under the weight of the motorcycle, the pain made her nauseated.

Freddie was slowly getting to his feet. His head was seeping blood again, but otherwise he seemed to be all right, only dazed. He said, "Are you all right?" and in the same moment noticed the wheel. "Oh, God," he said. He lifted it off her. "Can you move it? Is it busted?"

"I think so." She tried to sit up. "Maybe just sprained." She looked at it. It was swelling.

He looked around. Just beyond where they had fallen, there was a row of houses. He picked her up gently, frowning. "Am I hurting you?"

"No." It did hurt, though.

He carried her, as if she weighed nothing. At the first house, he rang the doorbell. A young woman opened the door.

"Oh, my goodness," she said. "You had an accident."

"Can I bring her in and call a doctor? She's broken her ankle, I think."

"Of course you can. But why don't I take you to Emergency at the hospital? It's just a few blocks away. The doctors are likely to be all out, at the hospital or over to Galveston helping out. They got hit real bad over there."

"We know. We were coming from there." Marcie felt silly, being held in Freddie's arms, but she was also grateful.

"Oh, bless your hearts. Wait, I'll get the car."

In a minute she had them on the way to the hospital. "We've been listening on the radio. It was bad here, but it's always worse over there. They say nobody got killed, praise God, but lots of damage, and people hurt. Here we are. I'll run in and tell them you're coming."

They had to wait, but not long. A young doctor sent Marcie

into X-ray, and then put a cast on her leg that reached almost to her knee.

"It's a simple break," he said. "Just be careful and you won't have any trouble. Come back in about six weeks and we'll take that thing off. You better use crutches for about ten days, and don't jump off any cliffs."

He spoke to the nurse, who got her some rental crutches and showed her how to use them.

Mrs. Benson, the woman who had brought them to the hospital, was waiting. Freddie had told her what their situation was, and she suggested that Marcie wait at her house until Freddie got the rental car and went back for the others. "You can put the motorcycle in our garage till you get back. It didn't get broken, did it?"

"I don't think so," Freddie said. "Maybe a dent or two."

She dropped him off at the car rental agency and took Marcie home with her. While they waited for Freddie and the others, Mrs. Benson made breakfast, and Marcie practiced walking with her crutches. The ankle didn't hurt much, just a dull ache, as long as she was careful not to put any weight on it. What a dumb thing to have happen! She wondered what her mother's reaction would be. Only she wouldn't be able to go to the Driskill. The doctor said she could drive, but he'd suggested waiting a few days. She'd better call her mother and prepare her. And Eric's family ought to be told he was all right. She decided to call Peg and ask her to let all of them know. That would be just one call.

She used Mrs. Benson's phone and reversed the charges to Peg.

"I've been so worried about you," Peg said. "But John said Freddie would get you all out safely."

"He did. I busted my ankle, and I look like the walking

wounded from some war movie, but it isn't bad. I got fixed up at the hospital. So don't worry. But will you alert Mom that I won't make it for dinner? And Eric's mother will be worrying."

"I know. She's called me three times already. Okay, Sis, I'll take care of it. Have you got a way to get home?"

"Freddie's renting a car."

"Have him bring you here. We'll give you the royal invalid treatment."

"All right, Peg. Thanks. See ya."

Marcie had begun to think of Mrs. Benson as an old friend by the time Freddie returned. Abner retrieved his BMW from the garage, while Freddie helped Marcie into the front seat of the rented Buick. Eric and Annie Guardino were so impressed with her cast, she began to feel like the heroine of some battle.

Abner, though grieving over a dent in the side of his beloved bike, offered Annie a ride to Houston. She was visibly thrilled. They took off, and a moment later Freddie, Eric, and Marcie were on their way home.

"That," Eric said, "was a music festival I'll never forget."

## 26

Freddie helped her up the front steps of the small house that John and Peg had bought on Wellington Road. Steps were hard to manage with the crutches. Peg and John were out on the porch to help her, too, as soon as they heard the car drive up, and Eric was standing behind so she wouldn't lose her balance.

"Boy, this is the most dramatic homecoming I ever had," Marcie said. "I should break a bone more often."

Peg looked unnecessarily concerned, Marcie thought. "It's just a simple fracture," she said. "I'd really be up a tree if it had been my wrist, but I don't need a working ankle to play the guitar."

Freddie was explaining to John. "I made arrangements with

a gas station guy to tow the van in as soon as he can get out there, but I'm going back first thing in the morning. It's got my guitars and my mandolin and Eric's clarinet and our sleeping bags and all kinds of stuff. Too tempting for thieves."

"Let me know if you have any problems," John said. "In fact, want me to go with you?"

"No, no, thanks, it'll be okay. Thanks a lot." He kissed the top of Marcie's head. "Take care, you hear?"

"Get something done about that gash on your head."

"All right. See y'all." And he and Eric left.

Marcie was surprised to find Nana in Peg's living room. She looked pale and unusually subdued.

"Honey, I'm so sorry," she said.

"It's all right, really. It doesn't even hurt. I've got some codeine if it starts to. It's just a simple fracture."

Peg had coffee and liverwurst sandwiches ready a few minutes after Marcie got there. It was about nine o'clock and Marcie was really tired .The food tasted good. But she couldn't understand why they all still looked so worried.

"I'm sorry you had to worry about the hurricane. I suppose it sounded awful on the radio or the TV. I wish I could have called you sooner. You explained to Mom why I didn't show up for dinner, didn't you?"

Peg bit her lip. She looked at John and then at Nana.

Marcie felt a surge of anxiety. "What's wrong?"

Nana came and sat beside her and took her hand. "Everything is all right, but your mother gave us a scare."

"What'd she do?"

"Well, it's my fault." Nana looked away for a moment. "As usual, I guess."

"Nana," Peg said, "don't."

162

"All right. I went to early church with your mother, and when we got back to the hotel, we had breakfast and then I told her I wanted to have a talk with her."

"Oh-oh," Marcie said.

"Yes, you could say that. I laid it on the line. I told her she was going to ruin your life if she didn't go on home and leave you alone."

Marcie clenched her teeth. She knew Nana had done it for her, but she wished she hadn't. "And I suppose she got a headache and an earache and went to bed, and what do we do now?"

"More than that, I'm afraid. She took an overdose of sleeping pills."

"What!" Marcie forgot her broken foot. She sat forward, brought her heel down on the floor, and felt a stab of pain. "Where is she?" She tried to get up.

"She's all right, Marcie. Sit down." It was John. He forced her gently back onto the sofa. Peg was crying. "Look, let me finish this story. I'm not involved, so I can tell you about it without dissolving into guilt. I do not think she meant to kill herself. I truly do not. She didn't take enough for that, and I have a hunch she was sure not to. After she took them, she called Peg and told her what she had done. Peg and I rushed her to the hospital and they pumped out her stomach. I don't mean to be unkind, but I think it was another one of her acts. Of course it could have backfired. If we hadn't been home, if she hadn't gotten hold of someone before she passed out, the pills might really have done the trick. It's hard to know how much it takes."

Marcie felt sick. "Where is she now?"

"At the hospital. They'll keep her overnight."

"Hadn't I better go see her?"

"No. She's sleeping it off. You can see her tomorrow."

"She's threatened to do this a lot of times since Dad left, but I never took her seriously."

"I don't think this was serious either, except that it was mighty risky," John said.

"Does she know I broke my ankle?"

"No. All this happened before Peg had a chance to tell her. Not long after you called, in fact."

Peg mopped her face. "What are we going to do?"

Nana sat up straighter. "I'll tell you what I'm going to do. I'm going to take her on a trip, and then I'm going to take her home."

"You were going on your own trip, with Bridget."

"That can wait. Marian has been complaining about never getting to go anywhere. So we'll go somewhere. Wherever she wants. I'll take her."

"Oh, Nana," Marcie said, "you'll hate it."

"I owe her. I owe you all. Marian is always saying I never wanted a child. She's right, though I'm sorry it showed. I tried to do all the things you're supposed to do, but I was in love with Alec, and we were having such a wonderful life together, I resented having everything change. The travel stopped, the wonderful and I suppose irresponsible life stopped. And five years later Alec died. I think I never forgave Marian for those five years that I had to devote to her. It's too late to make up for it, but I'll do what I can."

"Nana." Marcie took a moment to organize what she wanted to say. "You're doing just what you've been telling me not to do. You're letting Mom make you feel guilty, and you're changing your life to accommodate her. In the first

164

place, it isn't necessary. You gave her a perfectly good childhood. If she wanted more love than you had to give, that's not your fault. In the second place, nothing you might do would ever be enough. Believe me, I know. It wouldn't satisfy that terrible hunger she has. Nobody can do that. You go on your trip with Bridget. I'll talk to Mom tomorrow. Once I get it through her head that I'm not going home, and I'm not going to spend my time here with her, she'll go." Marcie hoped she sounded more convinced than she felt. But it was the only way to go.

All of them were silent for a few minutes.

"Marcie is right," John said. "It'll take guts, but Marcie's got 'em. Let her do it her way."

"Marcie's always had to bear the brunt," Peg said.

"Peg, don't you start," Marcie said. "I bore it because I did. Nobody made me." Suddenly she began to laugh. "It's crazy. Look at us. Three grown women sitting here wallowing in guilt because one spoiled woman has manipulated us into it. Come on, let's forget it. I'll fix it up tomorrow. How about more coffee? Can I have another sandwich?"

John's face broke into a wide grin. "Atta girl. I'll make you the sandwich with my own two hands. I'm a better cook than your sister any day."

"Prove it," Marcie said.

# 27

 Marcie woke up, feeling the discomfort of the heavy cast on her leg. She had taken a codeine tablet when she went to bed, so she had slept; but every time she moved her leg, she half woke.

She looked around at Peg's guest room. It was pretty. Pink-and-silver striped wallpaper, white French-Provincial-type furniture, ruffled white curtains. It was not at all the way she would have done a room, but it was attractive. It made her feel feminine and pampered.

She thought about what she had to do today and wished she could turn over and go back to sleep. If only someone could wave a magic wand and transport her mother back to Massachusetts, with no repercussions.

She sighed and began the process of getting out of bed. The smell of coffee helped. John teased Peg about her cooking, but she did make super coffee.

The plan, made before they all went to bed last night, was that John and Nana would pick up Mom at the hospital and get her settled in her room. Then Peg would drive Marcie to the Driskill, and she would do her big scene. She prayed it would work. Most of all she had to remember to keep her cool. Be grownup. Don't get manipulated. Last night John had said, "There's a child in all of us. The child in you and the child in your mother have been interacting like mad. Now you, as an adult, have to try to get her adult self to listen."

It sounded easy, but he had never had to cope with Mom.

She wasn't supposed to take a shower. No shower for six weeks? Good grief! She did the best she could with a sponge bath, but it wasn't easy. Even brushing her teeth was a problem, trying to brace herself with one hand and brush with the other. This was going to be a long bore.

When she was dressed, she managed the distance to the kitchen. Peg had a small table in the window overlooking the patio.

"It really is a neat house," Marcie said.

Peg looked pleased. But she seemed so nervous, Marcie found herself getting calmer, just to keep Peg calm.

"Nana called, and so did John. Mom is in her room at the hotel. Nana says she looks very pale and wan, but that's probably because she hasn't put on her makeup. John doesn't have to bring the car home for us after all because Kate offered to drive us downtown."

"I didn't know she was back. Did she have a good honeymoon?"

Peg smiled. "Everybody has a good honeymoon, I guess. Yeah, she did. They went to Fredericksburg and ate good food and walked around and did all the other things you do on a honeymoon."

"Eating out is kind of hard for Kate. Finding what she can eat."

"Well, she seems to have managed. She sounded happy."

They made conversation during breakfast. Only once did they speak of their mother. Peg said, "You've got a lot of guts, Marcie. You make me feel like such a wimp."

"Cut it out," Marcie said. She didn't feel like dealing with Peg's self-accusations.

Kate came soon after breakfast. She was wearing new clothes, at least new to Marcie, light tan corduroy pants and a lilac cotton turtleneck jersey. The weather was surprisingly cool, perhaps something to do with the hurricane, Marcie thought. Kate was full of sympathy for the broken ankle and the mother problem, but she was having trouble not looking radiantly happy.

Marcie asked questions about Fredericksburg on the way downtown, partly because she really wanted to hear Kate talk in that animated way and partly to keep her mind off what she had to do.

At the hotel, when Kate had found a parking space, Peg said, with obvious reluctance, "Do you want me to go in with you?"

"Of course not. You and Kate go shop or something. It may take a while. Anyway I'll find you."

"I feel like such a heel," Peg said.

"Oh, Peg, do shut up," Marcie said.

Peg looked at Kate. "What do you do when your kid sister tells you to shut up?"

"You shut up," Kate said. She opened the passenger door and helped Marcie out. "Stay here, Peg. I'll be right back." She opened the door to the lobby and went with Marcie to the elevator. "Are you all right?" She held the elevator door.

"Sure."

"In case you want to know, I'm proud of you. I wish I could help."

"You've been helping ever since I met you. I've got my own super support group now. You, John, Manuel, Freddie, Eric, Abner, Nana, Aunt Meg, even my big sister. I can do it. I think." She waved at Kate and let the elevator door close.

I think, I think, I think, she said to herself, as she got out of the elevator and made her slow way down the corridor to her mother's room. She knocked twice before she heard the faint, "Come in." The door was unlocked. Her mother was in bed, wearing a new bed jacket. Bought for the occasion? Marcie thought, and then reminded herself not to be bitchy. She approached the bed. "Hi, Mom."

Her mother was staring at her in horror. "What on earth! Mother said you hurt your foot, but I had no idea. Marcie, you need taking care of."

Marcie was prepared for this. "Not in the least. I have a very minor break. It just looks bad, because it has to be immobilized for a while. Actually it's kind of interesting. I get all sorts of attention. Remember when you broke your arm?"

"But I could walk."

"So can I."

"People never tell me anything."

Marcie let herself down carefully on the foot of the bed. "I'm glad you're feeling better. It was a foolish, dangerous thing you did, and I hope you never do anything like that again."

Her mother stuck out her lower lip in her hurt-child look. "I was in despair. Nobody cares about me. I'm no use to anyone."

As briskly as she could, Marcie said, "That's nonsense, and you know it. Your trouble is, you're homesick. And I don't blame you a bit. You're missing all your friends. Do you realize the church fair is just ten days away? They've never been able to put together a decent fair without you. Mabel Woodson and the Bedell sisters and Mrs. Fairbanks . . . you know how much they depend on you."

Her mother gave a smug little smile. "Well, Mabel is such a scatterbrain."

"Father Goodhue is probably having a fit, wondering why you don't come home and get with it. I mean he doesn't even have his wife—"

"Oh, that woman. She never lifted a finger."

"So it's really up to you, Mom. I know you won't feel right about staying away. If you left tomorrow, you'd be there in plenty of time to straighten things out."

Her mother looked at her suspiciously. "You're just trying to get rid of me. You and Mother."

"Don't be silly. You're bored stiff here, and you know it."

"Well, it's such a terrible climate. So hot. And I don't know anyone. Even that Duplessis woman broke her engagement with me yesterday."

"You need your own good friends. The bridge clubs are probably in a mess without you."

"I'm entitled to a vacation, after all."

"Sure you are, and you've had one. Think of all the stories you'll have to tell. I'll call the Harwood travel people and book you for tomorrow, if you think you feel well enough. We can have dinner together tonight."

"I can't leave you in this crippled condition."

"Mom, I'm getting more attention than I need."

"That's not the same as your mother's care. You think you're so independent, Marcie, but you need me."

"Sure I do, Mom, but not twenty-four hours a day, right? Listen, I was thinking about Christmas. What if we forget all that home stuff—I mean the tree and all that jazz. Let's meet in New York and stay at the Pierre and go to the theater and eat a lot of outrageous meals in wonderful restaurants. What do you say?"

In spite of herself her mother's face lit up. "That does sound like fun. Just you and me?"

"Just you and me."

"Because I don't want Mother there, lecturing me."

"Just us."

"Well, all right. Maybe you'll get sick of Austin and come home sooner."

"If I do, you'll be the first to know. That's a joke, Mom; laugh."

Her mother gave her a wan smile.

Marcie picked up the phone book, found the travel agency number, and dialed it before her mother could say anything more. She got her a flight for the following morning.

"It's an easy connection at Dallas," she said when she had hung up. "An hour between flights, so you don't have to hurry. You'll get into Logan at four thirty-five. Why don't I

171

phone somebody to meet you? Janice Fuller is always driving into Boston . . ."

"No, I think I'll take a taxi. I've always wanted to take a taxi all the way from Logan home. I think I'll do it. After all, I'm not feeling terribly strong."

"I think that's a great idea. I'll phone Mrs. McGraw and ask her to open up the house, air it out a bit."

"She'll see how dusty it is."

"Of course it's dusty; you haven't been there." She was doing her best to answer all these silly arguments without sounding impatient.

"All right. Tell her to open the upstairs windows, not the downstairs. I don't want anyone breaking in."

"I'll tell her." Marcie stood up and picked up her crutches.

"Oh, Marcie, my poor baby. How are you going to get home?"

If she said Peg and Kate had brought her, that would bring on a new argument. She rolled her eyes and said, "I have vays!"

"Nobody even told me how it happened."

"A tiny accident on the road. A freak accident. Don't worry your head about it." She kissed her mother's cheek. "Can I help you pack?"

"Oh no. I'll manage somehow. You'll be here for dinner?"

"You bet." She hoped it wasn't a mistake, that her mother wouldn't have had time to think up new arguments for not going home, but it seemed the least she could do. "Be thinking where you'd like to go. I'll buy."

"Oh just downstairs, I think. Neither of us is up to going out. Maybe we could have room service."

"Fine with me. I'll see you around seven."

When she was out in the corridor, she leaned against the wall. suddenly weak. It had worked. So far. So far.

172

Kate and Peg were waiting for her in the lobby. She made a circle with her thumb and forefinger. "We have to pick up her plane ticket at Harwood's."

"Good girl," Kate said.

# 28

 Freddie came to see her when he got back from Galveston. He phoned ahead so she could take her time getting to the door and unlocking it. Freddie thought of everything.

"It was bloody but unbowed," he said in answer to her question about the van. "Or more accurately, muddy but unmolested . . . The gas station guy cleaned it up for me. Nice guy. Dried out the muck in the engine and all that. It was mostly just water. How you feelin'?"

"Free." She told him about her mother.

"Was the parting at the airport bloody?"

"No, she wouldn't let any of us go with her. She took a taxi to the airport and flew off all by herself. I guess it was easier for her that way. It was certainly easier on me." She shook her head. "Right now I'm worrying my fool head off."

He went into the kitchen and dumped out a bag of lemons he had brought. "Make you some lemonade." When he came back, he said, "Of course you worry. She's your old lady after all, and you do love her."

"Yes, I do." She was glad he'd said that. Everybody had been so busy telling her how to live without her mother, nobody had stopped to think that Marcie loved the woman. Otherwise she would have cut out long ago, the way Peg had. "I guess I just needed to learn about tough love, as they say. Like not letting your kids walk all over you, no matter how much you love 'em."

He opened up a section of a Houston newspaper that he'd had in his hip pocket. "Take a look."

There was a very good picture of Abner grinning at Annie Guardino. The caption read AUSTIN MAN RESCUES LOCAL WOMAN IN HURRICANE. And there was a brief story about Abner saving Annie on his motorcycle.

"That's nice," Marcie said. "She did say her boyfriend was on the paper. It makes Abner sound like a knight on horseback."

"Only Abner's going to have a man-sized fit. He's been doing his best to keep a low profile, and here he is plastered all over the paper."

"Oh. That's right."

"Personally I don't believe the U.S. Navy is spending all its resources tracking down one sailor that split. Especially one that was in sick bay at the time. But Abner's paranoid about it. He'll probably change his name and move again."

"We've got to do something about Abner."

"Yeah. But what?"

"I was thinking, and maybe this gives us the excuse, I'd like to get him together with Manuel."

"He doesn't need a lawyer, he needs a shrink."

"All right, but Manuel sends some of his people to the Mental Health Clinic. He works with people who are really down-and-out, and a lot of them need help like that. He knows the Clinic people. If we could get them together, and I could brief Manuel ahead of time, maybe on the basis of helping Abner in case of legal problems . . . oh, I don't know, I don't know enough about all that . . . but I have a feeling if anybody could get Abner to feel safe about getting psychological help, it would be Manuel."

"Okay, let's do it soon. Abner may get scared enough to disappear, if he hasn't already. I have an excuse to call him. Harry at Po'Boy's wants us to do another gig. Would you feel like it next Saturday? I told him you busted your ankle." Freddie grinned. "He said they could autograph your cast. Not," he added, "that I recommended that."

"Saturday would be great."

"I'll call Ab now."

Marcie sipped her lemonade and thought about how good she felt, while Freddie called Abner.

When he came back, he said, "He's running scared, like I expected. He won't play at Harry's, but that's all right. I know another guy we can get. I told him about Manuel; Ab's met him, of course. I said you thought Manuel could get him out of any jam he might get into. He said he'd talk to him. So you talk to Manuel, okay? I told Ab to call me in the morning, and we'd tell him when and where." He sat down and stretched his long legs out in front of him. "Abner can be a pain, but he's worth saving."

The phone rang, and this time it was Nana.

"All went well?" she said.

"Fine, Nana. Thanks for your moral support. I may need it again later. This stuff takes time."

"You were a lot braver than I've ever been," Nana said. Then in her old jubilant voice she said, "Bridget and I got our tickets this morning. Buenos Aires for a week, and then a week on a divine little British Caribbean island called Montserrat. It has a rain forest and an extinct volcano . . . at least they *say* it's extinct, but with my luck it will probably blow." She sounded as if she meant with her good luck, it would blow.

Marcie laughed. "And you've never seen a volcano go off, and what's life without at least one volcano?"

"Exactly. I missed Kilauea twice. *Twice* it went off right after Alec and I had left Hawaii. Darling, I'll send you post cards. Take care of your ankle. And above all, *enjoy!*"

Marcie hung up, smiling. "My grandmother says I'm to enjoy."

"All right, my girl, but there's work ahead too, you know." He went to the door. "Hold the fort. I'll be right back."

"Where are you going?"

"Down to the van. I've got a little present for you."

He came back carrying his own Martin and another one that Marcie had never seen. "While I was in Houston, I went into a shop to check out the guitars. I got me some new strings, and while I was there, I saw this . . ." He held out the other Martin. "It's old, and it sounds good. You've messed around with that Yamaha long enough."

"Freddie!" She couldn't think of anything else to say. She tuned the guitar and hit a few chords. It sounded mellow and wonderful. "What can I say? I'd rather have this than any-

177

thing in the world. How can I thank you?" She was afraid she was going to cry, and Freddie would hate that.

He took his own guitar out of the case, trying to look stern, but his face shone with pleasure. He struck his introductory chord and went into a fast, sure "Sweet Georgia Brown."

With a grin that she could feel stretching right across her face, Marcie picked up her guitar and joined him. It was going to be a year, all right.